HOW DOES A SINGLE BLADE OF GRASS THANK THE SUN?

Doretta Lau

How does a single blade of grass thank the sun?

NIGHTWOOD EDITIONS

2014

Nightwood Editions
P.O. Box 1779
Gibsons, BC von 1v0
Canada
www.nightwoodeditions.com

TYPOGRAPHY & COVER DESIGN: Carleton Wilson

Nightwood Editions acknowledges financial support from the Government of Canada through the Canada Book Fund and the Canada Council for the Arts, and from the Province of British Columbia through the British Columbia Arts Council and the Book Publisher's Tax Credit.

This book has been produced on 100% post-consumer recycled, ancient-forest-free paper, processed chlorine-free and printed with vegetable-based dyes.

Printed and bound in Canada.

LIBRARY AND ARCHIVES CANADA CATALOGUING IN PUBLICATION

Lau, Doretta, author
How does a single blade of grass thank the sun? / Doretta Lau.

Short stories.
ISBN 978-0-88971-293-5 (pbk.)

I. Title.

PS8623.A8165H69 2014   C813'.6   C2014-900621-7

For Mom and Dad

Contents

God Damn, How Real Is This?

MY FUTURE SELF SENDS me a text message at least once a day.

The latest: HEY, TRICHO-SLUT, GET YOUR MAN HANDS OUT OF OUR HAIR. I HAVE A LAKE MICHIGAN–SHAPED BALD SPOT FORMING ON THE BACK OF MY HEAD. STOP PLUCKING. IT'S STARTING TO LOOK LIKE A PENIS.

Last I checked there were no Great Lakes of any sort blooming on my scalp, no Superiors or Hurons or Eries flooding my hair. Of late, these missives from the future have become increasingly more abusive. I wonder, when will I flip my bitch switch and hop on this negative self-talk train? In a week? In a year? I'd like to believe this use of misogynistic language is out of character and that maybe I'm being trolled by a bored identity thief. I file the thought as something for my present self to discuss with my now therapist.

Another message flashes on my phone: THAT MOLE ON YOUR LEFT ARM THAT YOU'VE BEEN IGNORING? GET THEE TO A DOCTOR.

I peer down. My arm is presenting itself as blemish free. At times like this I wish I could send a text to my future self to make clear the murky. I want to address important issues such as: will I die alone? But that technology hasn't been invented yet, or our future selves have circumvented its implementation for the good of humanity.

I call my local clinic and explain my situation.

"This is Franny Siu calling. I can't find this mole my future self is warning me about, but I'd like to make an appointment to see Doctor Chang."

"I understand," says the woman on the phone. "Last week, my future self started blasting me messages about herpes. Today, she escalated to drug-resistant gonorrhea. I think she's trying to tell me that my boyfriend is cheating on me."

"No sex for the hexed," I say, unsure how to handle this kind of intimacy with a near stranger.

"Come at two tomorrow afternoon."

"Great. See you tomorrow," I say, and hang up.

Despite this disruption, I still have time before my therapy session to stop by my ex-colleague Rita's house and check on her. Rita has not left her house in months because her future self keeps divining death and destruction. As soon as she thinks of doing something—innocuous activities such as watching a movie or washing her feet—a new text arrives dissuading her from taking action.

I pack up some leftover food and a stack of library books, slap SPF 90 sunscreen on my face and arms, and get on my bike. A block from Rita's, I see that Chronology Purists have purchased a new billboard: HAS COMMUNICATIVE TIME TRAVEL RUINED YOUR LIFE? OUR COUNSELLORS ARE READY TO TALK.

I think about calling the number listed, but decide instead to stop at a convenience store to pick up additional supplies.

The scene indoors is vaguely apocalyptic. The lights are off. Many shelves gape, emptied of goods. Since the texts from the future began arriving nine months earlier, people have been hoarding canned food and toilet paper out of fear that the new technology has sparked end times. I sigh. Spoiler alert, present-day peons: it's our appalling behaviour that blights our existence.

I grab a loaf of bread and head to the counter. The clerk is wearing a bulletproof vest.

"What if I shot you in the head?" I ask. "The vest wouldn't do you much good then."

"Do you think you're the first to ask that, smartass? My future self has already pointed that out to me, thank you very much," he says.

"How does the store stay afloat without the scratch-and-wins?" I ask, motioning to the bare strip of space under the Plexiglas countertop. Three months ago, the government suspended all forms of gambling. I miss the surprise of running a toonie across a scratch card, that sick joy of self-inflicted failure that's preceded ever so briefly by hope.

"That will be ten dollars, please," he says, pointing to the bread.

I REACH RITA'S HOUSE and speak through the front door. "Hey, I'm leaving you some gazpacho. The ingredients are organic. I triple-filtered the water. There's also a loaf of gluten-free bread and the books you asked for."

No answer. The smell of feet lingers in the air.

"Just send me a text," I say.

My phone pings with a message from present-Rita: THANKS, FRANNY. THERE'S TWENTY BUCKS FOR YOU UNDER THE DOORMAT AND A BOOK THAT NEEDS TO BE RETURNED.

"Your recent actions are fashioning me into an enabler," I say, stooping down to look under the mat. "I don't like who I am becoming under your influence."

No answer.

I text her: YOUR FUTURE SELF IS CHICKEN LITTLE. YOUR FUTURE SELF HAS BECOME YOUR MOTHER.

No response. I move on.

MY THERAPIST, KELLY, DOES not have a cellphone. She's a Chronology Purist—she wants her life to play out exactly as it would have if communicative time travel had not been invented. I don't get how this is possible, given that the timeline has already been breached, but logic is not my strong suit so maybe I'm missing the point. Sometimes her future self tries to get in touch with her via my phone, but present-Kelly has instructed me never to pass on any information. I'm in the uncomfortable position of knowing that the majority of her stocks will tank in the next six months...though I suppose if I do pass on the information, it would be classified as insider trading. I keep my mouth shut; we both stay out of jail. I wonder if I should look for a new therapist.

"How was your week?" Kelly asks.

"I worry that I am a misogynist," I say. "My future self is really fond of calling me a slut or a whore, which I find puzzling because I never use either of those words. I'd be much more likely to refer to myself as a douchebag."

"What at present do you think is causing this negativity?"

"I don't know. I'm frustrated with the fact that I can't communicate with my future self. I mean, I guess I could leave notes for her in my journal, but I don't know if she'll ever see them."

"What can you do right now that will make you feel better?"

"I guess I could write a letter to myself, and you can give it back to me six months later."

"Okay, do you want to try that this week?"

"Yes," I say.

"Our time is up," she says, standing. "Until next week."

As soon I leave the office, a new message arrives from my future self: HEY RICKETS BREATH, HAVE YOU TAKEN YOUR CALCIUM AND VITAMIN-D SUPPLEMENT TODAY?

I hit delete.

Kelly's future self is angry with me: I'M GOING TO HAVE TO RAISE MY FEES TO COVER MY LOSSES, SO YOU'RE THE ONE WHO WILL SUFFER IF YOU DON'T TELL ME TO SELL THE STOCK.

I decide to write two letters: one to my future self and one to Kelly's.

THE NEXT DAY AT the doctor's office, the waiting room is a cacophony of phones beeping and bleeping. Everyone looks anxious. I know now that ignorance is Eden. If I knew how to code a virus, I would direct my future self to send the inventor of communicative time travel a diseased email to avert this reality.

I text Wilson to meet me at 2:30 at a coffee shop across from the clinic—I need someone to talk to in case I have terminal cancer—and he replies with an immediate affirmative.

The receptionist, who does not look ill, calls my name and leads me to a private room.

Doctor Chang appears after a few minutes. He examines my arm and says, "Do you think that maybe—and I don't want to sound judgmental—that your future self suffers from a touch of Münchausen by proxy?"

"What makes you say that?"

"You've been here seven times during this past month. You complain of future ailments, but in actuality they're merely imaginary diseases foisted upon you by your future self."

"I read somewhere that the child is the father of the man," I say.

"Are you still pulling your hair out?"

"Did my future self contact you about that?"

"Yes."

"I'm sorry we have no boundaries," I say. "Also, isn't my condition just Münchausen? I mean, I'm still me, even in the future. No proxy."

Doctor Chang gives me a look that indicates that he is the medical professional and I am just a poor excuse for a patient.

I leave his office in shame. My diagnosis? Dormant Münchausen by proxy.

WILSON IS LATE FOR our meeting at the coffee shop. My hand wanders to my tresses.

My phone pings. WHOREBAG! PLACE YOUR MAN HANDS WHERE I CAN SEE THEM OR I'LL SHOOT!

I sigh and fold my hands in my lap. The last thing I need is for my future self to become suicidal and send an assassin my way.

Fifteen minutes, three hairs and four text messages later, Wilson rolls in on a skateboard.

"*Konichiwa*," he says, kissing me on the cheek. "Nice dress."

"Those wheels become less and less an acceptable form of transportation with each passing calendar year," I say to him.

"I broke up with Cynthia," he says with a shrug. "I live for today."

Two months ago, Wilson's future self went silent. No texts or email. He concluded that his future self was dead, so his motto became *carpe diem*. He made a bucket list, which included things such as climb Mount Everest, learn Japanese and eat yogurt for the first time ever. Everest was a bust (summit, avalanche) and he's lactose intolerant. I suspect this list could be the reason for his early demise, but I haven't said anything because I don't want to be a killjoy.

"Did you get a haircut?" I ask.

"I did—that's why I was late. So, how did your appointment go?"

"My doctor says I have dormant Münchausen by proxy but I think it may just be plain Münchausen since I'm doing it to myself," I say. "There's now a hold on my insurance for a month and I can only seek medical help in life or death situations. Also, Rita still won't leave her house."

"Forget your troubles. I'm here! Come to the park with me," Wilson says, grabbing my hand.

"Is there a cliff you want to jump off?"

"Something like that. Better, actually. Also, I stopped drinking coffee and I don't like the way they serve tea here."

"What's better than jumping off a cliff?" I ask.

"You'll see," he says, smiling.

We leave on our separate vehicles. I reach the park first. Wilson shows up with a fresh bruise on his arm.

"I fell," he says. "I wish my future self were alive so he could send warnings."

"Everyone is afraid to live now," I say. "You should be thankful for the radio silence."

"I'm nearly done everything on my list. There's only one thing left."

"What is it?" I ask.

He points to something in the trees. I gaze up in search of this final thing, sure that I'm about to witness some new kind of beauty, but I don't see anything. When I look back at Wilson his face has travelled and is inches from mine. He kisses me. I close my eyes and think only of the present.

We separate. He smiles.

"I feel the same way about you, too," I say.

His phone pings. A look of surprise lights up his face. "It's a text from my future self."

YOU MAGNIFICENT BASTARD, it reads. I'M GLAD YOU STOPPED

BEING A SCARED LITTLE PANSY AND CHOSE TO LIVE LIFE. DON'T FUCK THIS UP FOR US. I LOVE HER.

He turns off his phone, but not before I glimpse the rest of the message.

TELL HER TO GET THAT MOLE ON HER LEFT ARM CHECKED.

Two-Part Invention

I

THE NEIGHBOURS WHO LIVE in the apartment above mine are having loud sex. Our building has thin walls and creaky floors. Every Sunday, they follow the same routine. They throw on a Sarah McLachlan album. The man likes to talk—too much, in my opinion. They get straight down to business, as if they are in a movie where the woman doesn't need foreplay. Their moaning and panting never exceeds the length of the album. Sometimes I wonder why their record collection is so small. Why haven't they purchased any new music since 1997?

I'm aware of their schedule because every Sunday at 7 P.M. my grandmother Nina calls me.

The phone rings. I answer it without hesitation. "Hello," I say.

"Are you watching porn?" Nina asks.

"I don't have a TV," I tell her. "I'm not watching porn."

"I can hear it. You're watching porn. If you're lonely, just admit it. There's nothing to be ashamed of. It's perfectly healthy."

"I am *not* watching porn." I try to keep my voice even and respectful.

"Why haven't you found a man?" she asks.

"A good man is hard to find," I say, trying not to sigh. I feel no need to come up with a witty or original answer because she asks this question every time she calls, after she has inquired whether I have eaten. Even if I haven't eaten, I always tell her that I did indeed eat. I know it makes her happy if I am not hungry.

"My doctor is a fine young man. I believe he's single," she says, excited.

"Sounds like you have a little crush on him. Are you going to ask him out?"

"Silly! He's perfect for *you*. I'm happy to be single. I don't want another man now that your grandfather has passed. Besides, I've had my share of boyfriends. They were all older men and now most of them are dead."

"Really?" I say. "This gives me a brilliant idea."

I HAVE DECIDED TO date dead men.

"So silly!" Nina says when I tell her my plan the following Sunday. "Your parents wasted good money sending you to school. No common sense."

"There are more dead men than living men."

"I suppose you have a point." She sighs. "Is it possible that a dead man will father my great-grandchildren?"

AFTER SOME THOUGHT, I decide that I would like to go on a date with Alain Delon, but when I tell Nina this she tells me he's not dead. "Too bad," I say.

I start reading biographies because I often find answers in books. Before my decision to find a dead man, I read only fiction. I read stories about unhappy people. Somehow, this made me happy. Now, the unhappy people I read about were once alive. This does not make me feel particularly happy at all.

"Why are you only considering movie stars?" Nina asks me when she hears that my reading list consists only of actor biographies. "And Bruce Lee! He was still married when he died and his wife is alive! Are you going to be an adulterer? Your parents raised you to behave better than this."

"I believe his wife has since remarried. Twice."

Nina is silent for a moment. "And Ruan Lingyu is a woman!"

"I liked her performance in *The Goddess*. She's a Chinese film icon. I want to meet her."

"Is this why you don't want to find a man? You like women. Is that it?"

I laugh. "If I liked women, I wouldn't be searching for a dead man."

I KNOW THE MEN I am considering are dead, but still I fear rejection. What if they wish only to date the dead? I'm not willing to die for a man.

Days go by. My search proves to be difficult. I have trouble making decisions when presented with numerous choices. Sometimes I think I would thrive in a Communist state, or in an arranged marriage. I do well when there are limitations and boundaries.

"Why not historical figures?" Nina asks.

"Who do you have in mind?"

"Genghis Khan."

"Too brutal."

"Malcolm X."

"He was still married when he was assassinated. And his wife never remarried. Plus, she's been dead for some time. I imagine they're back together."

"Li Bai."

"I should read his poetry." I add him to my list.

"Einstein."

"I'd feel stupid."

Then we're silent. It seems wrong to make specific demands of dead men when I'm not perfect myself. All I want is someone similar to me in taste and temperament, but who is a better person than me in every way.

"I was never good at history in school," Nina says. "Forget I said anything."

THAT NIGHT, AS I scan through my bookcases, I think about the pianist Glenn Gould, who was as strange as he was talented: first he was young and played Bach so quickly people had to reconsider Bach.

Later, when he was older and played Bach more carefully, people had to reconsider Gould.

I START READING ABOUT Gould and discover that most texts focus on a few key personal traits. Often, he thought he was succumbing to illness. He had an aversion to human contact—he especially disliked having his hands touched. Near the end of his life, his hypochondria exceeded even his genius. He lined his bathroom cabinet with row upon row of prescription medication. Many of the pills were incompatible. Nine days after his fiftieth birthday, he died from complications arising from a stroke.

Nina approves of Glenn Gould, though she calls him an eccentric. She cannot understand why, at age thirty-two—the height of his career as a concert pianist—he gave up performing to concentrate solely on recording. At first the recording sessions took place in New York, but later Gould preferred to use the Eaton Auditorium in Toronto.

"He was always cold, even in hottest summer," she tells me. "He soaked his hands in scalding water before playing. And he recommended dipping the hands into hot paraffin to relieve bursitis."

This revelation makes me feel closer to Gould. Although it is not genius, we have something in common. "I often soak my arms in hot and cold water to help my poor circulation," I say. I have a repetitive stress injury in both arms, but not from being a famous pianist. I did play once, but not well. I spent too much time typing and now it hurts to shake hands when meeting new people. When the pain was at its worst, I couldn't open doors or read heavy books. All I wanted to do was watch television and withdraw from any activity that involved using my hands. I sold my piano.

NINA SENDS ME A crate of Glenn Gould records and a copy of Thomas Bernhard's novel *The Loser*. I lie on my couch and listen to each record twice. Every note is an analog wonder. I do not leave my apartment for two days and read *The Loser* out loud to myself.

I call Nina to thank her.

"When I listen to Glenn Gould play, I feel young again," she says.

She has said the same thing of Paul Anka, George Gershwin, Tom Jones and the soundtrack for *The Sound of Music*.

I am unsure whether my search for a dead man is over.

ANDREW KAZDIN, GOULD'S PRODUCER from 1965 to 1979, wrote the biography *Glenn Gould at Work: Creative Lying*. The book is as much about Kazdin as it is about Gould. This is okay. When I think about Gould, I start thinking about myself as well.

My favourite anecdote from the biography is about coffee rather than music. During a recording session in Toronto, Gould requested a coffee with two sugars and two creams. More specifically, he asked for a *double double*, a phrase commonly used in eastern Canada. One can also order a *triple triple* or *four by four*. Kazdin, an American, had never heard the term before and thought it yet another of the pianist's eccentricities. Even when he heard the words *double double* on television years later, he still thought that Gould had coined the phrase.

THE DAY AFTER I finish reading *Glenn Gould at Work: Creative Lying*, Nina calls me even though it isn't Sunday.

"I guess you're not as lonely now," she says.

"Why do you say that?"

"You're not watching porn."

I ignore this statement. "I just finished reading another book about Gould."

"Which one?"

"The one by Andrew Kazdin."

"It's filled with firsthand information, but it lacks a certain something, doesn't it?"

"Yeah, but I can't quite figure out what it is," I say. "Perhaps I want only fictions and fakery." I think for a moment. "But I like knowing that Gould wanted the wires in his Steinway so tight that sometimes the hammers in the piano fired twice, causing ghost notes."

THE NEXT WEEK I read a story by John Haskell, which begins: "Glenn Gould had a thing about microphones. Not a bad thing; he loved them and loved using them, as long as they weren't in front of people." Although I like these sentences, from what I understand Gould didn't so much dislike performing in front of people as he wanted every audience member to have a similar experience of his playing. In an auditorium, this was out of his control. Some seats are better than others, near to the stage, or in the row where sound is as close to perfection as a room can allow. But in a recording studio, he could spend days on the same piece, creating a performance that could be experienced repeatedly and in a similar fashion by many people. He may have felt as a pianist he was playing for the audience, but as a recording artist he was playing for himself.

Lydia Davis wrote my favourite of all lines about Gould: "He sometimes practised with the vacuum cleaner on because that way, he said, he could hear the skeleton of the music." The essence of his strangeness and genius are revealed in this line; Davis has gotten at who Gould is in a single sentence, while several writers have filled pages and still cannot wholly describe what separated him from other virtuoso musicians.

I run my vacuum and listen to Gould's 1981 interpretation of the *Goldberg Variations*, hoping that the skeleton of the music will appear to me as obvious as a dinosaur fossil display in a museum of natural history.

I THINK OF DATE possibilities. Perhaps he can give me a piano lesson.

I imagine this: I am seated at a piano, on a bench, while Gould is in a comfortable chair that's quite low to the ground. During this first lesson he doesn't let me touch the piano, nor does he touch it himself. We listen to recordings of his work and I sit with the scores before me, taking notes. Gould tells me that he doesn't want me to interpret the work in the same way. We are two different people. Plus, I do not possess the level of virtuosity necessary to mimic his playing style.

We spend the lesson talking about everything but music. He wants to know what I think about reality television, a concept he doesn't quite understand but finds fascinating.

I tell him about what he's missed since October 4, 1982.

"And people have chunks of the wall in their homes, as souvenirs?" he asks.

So much time has passed between his death and our date that I imagine I cannot fail to be interesting, if not charming.

II

I GET UP THE nerve to contact Glenn Gould to ask him if he would like to meet. I seek help from a famous medium; she charges me double the going rate because she feels I am degrading her profession by asking her to act as a glorified matchmaker.

To my surprise, Gould says yes. He is difficult even in death, refusing to meet me in Vancouver even though he could arrive by blinking or humming a few bars of a Schoenberg opera.

I agree to fly to Toronto. Gould doesn't want to dine in the city, for fear of being recognized. So we settle on a truck-stop diner forty-five minutes east of the city. I rent a car and navigate the expansive highway system with a map I purchased at the airport.

When I arrive at the restaurant, he is already seated at a booth. The heat is up high, yet he's got a long scarf wrapped thrice round his neck.

"Hello," I say, as he rises to greet me.

"Have a seat," he says.

I sit across from him. "You look just like the inside photograph in the booklet for *A State of Wonder*, the pinkish-toned one." I can tell that I am on the verge of incoherent rambling.

"I hate that picture. I look old there."

"You look like you're concentrating on something important."

"How was your trip here?"

"Oh, it wasn't bad. The flight wasn't full. I had three seats to myself." I am nervous. Due to my nerves, I am being boring. If I am not careful, I will start repeating what I have already said, something that happens to me when I'm nervous and cannot think of what to say.

Gould's menu is closed. He has already decided what he wants. I open my menu and order a hamburger and fries because it is a familiar meal and I am in an unfamiliar situation.

We do not speak. Until the food arrives, Gould hums a tune I don't recognize.

I start salting my food and say, "You were right to choose recording over performing."

"Yes?"

"Yes. With the recordings, it seems as though you are not dead. You are alive, again and again. On repeat. On the radio. In my apartment."

"A haunting?"

"You're there like the ghost notes Andrew Kazdin describes removing from your recordings."

"Interesting," he says. I don't know how to interpret this single word. There is no word more uninteresting than *interesting*. I'm anxious about the fact that he is answering with one or two words. I had read that he would talk for hours on end, without pausing to let the other person speak. And I know that he has a tendency to drop people from his life without explanation. Yet, I still want to connect to him as a person, rather than as an iconic figure.

"I gave it a lot of thought and I know why Bach of all the composers fits you best," I say.

"Yes?"

"Well, it strikes me that you have a tiring internal struggle, a war between not wanting to encounter people, to stay reclusive, but also wanting everyone's full attention. In Bach there's the contrapuntal constructions, notes that go in contrast without clashing, that hold together within the piece. His work exists because of contraries, as do you." I take a big bite of my hamburger and chew with purpose.

Gould has stopped eating and is looking at me. He starts humming the opening aria from the *Goldberg Variations*, at the tempo of his 1955 recording, quick.

When I put the burger down, and before I can reach for the napkin to remove the grease from my hands, Gould reaches his left hand out and clasps my right hand tightly. The gesture feels like ten hours of conversation, years of friendship. I remain still, even though it hurts.

Days of Being Wild

THAT FALL IN NEW YORK, most of my thoughts had to do with pain or grief. I was not suicidal. Rather, my grandmother had died a few months earlier and I was slowly recovering from the loss. I did not know how to talk about my pain, so I often drank until I could no longer feel my hands or feet. Insomnia took hold of me. I lay in bed and watched movies until 5 or 6 A.M., taking careful notes for the screenplay I was supposed to complete to attain my master's degree. Although four months had passed since the end of coursework, I was still working on the first act. No matter how many hours I sat in front of my computer, I could not advance the plot of the film. My characters were flat. Each line of dialogue I wrote felt like an affront to the English language.

Everyone I attracted during this time was equally preoccupied with various miseries. A Ph.D. history student who lived in my building, Kenichi Kingsley, considered me his only friend in the city. I am not sure what qualified me for this honour. I had not sought out his friendship, nor had I been particularly kind to him when we first met. To be honest, I had been wary of him because he was attractive in a movie-star sort of way. My mother had often warned me that beautiful men lacked a conscience.

Kenichi was on antidepressants, which made him an undesirable drinking companion—he was incomprehensibly drunk after only two beers. Yet, he insisted upon drinking with me on Thursday nights, after his course on the modern history of Japan. It was one of the few fixed appointments on my calendar. We always went to the same restaurant, and we always sat at the bar. Our friendship was a habit, like smoking or biting one's nails to the quick.

"I hate the guys in my class," Kenichi said, after a large gulp of beer. "Most of them have or want Japanese wives or girlfriends."

"Isn't that what you want, too? A girl like your mother?" It was easy for me to rile him because his fears were so similar to my own—we thought that we were doomed to become the sort of people we most despised.

"Shut up." He smacked my arm, hard.

"Is the seating in your class segregated? Does it feel like the South that Flannery O'Connor depicts in her stories, except with Asian protagonists?"

"If you're asking me where I sit—I sit with the Japanese kids." Kenichi scowled at me. He considered himself one hundred percent Japanese, though he had a British father whom he barely remembered. Kenichi had lived with his mother in Japan for most of his life and had attended boarding school in England. A few weeks after I met him, I entered the bathroom in his apartment and noticed that he had covered all the mirrors with vintage wallpaper. He later confessed that he couldn't bear to look at his reflection because he strongly resembled his father, whom he hated.

"I bet all the women in your class love you," I said. "You look like Daniel Henney or Dennis Oh."

"You watch too many Korean dramas."

"I'm attracted to tragedy."

"This is why we're friends."

I raised my shot of bourbon. "To tragedy."

We drained our glasses. Then we had another. As usual, Kenichi became a slurring mess once he finished his second beer.

"You have to catch up," he said, pushing my drink towards me. "Drink faster."

I was on my fourth bourbon. "Catch up? You're the one who's behind."

"You're not on meds." He began to slide down in his seat. "Because of the meds, I'm way ahead of you."

"Maybe you shouldn't drink."

He tried to sit up. He began staring at my face as if there was an answer to an important question on it. "You're the only person I know who isn't afraid to be unhappy."

I didn't know what to say. Wasn't unhappiness something sensible people avoided? Before I could answer, a woman leaned in between us, facing Kenichi, and asked, "What time is it?"

"Ask her," he said, pointing to me. "I'm not wearing a watch."

This was a lie. Kenichi was wearing a watch. I could see this, and so could the woman.

The woman didn't turn. She stepped closer to him; it was clear that she didn't care what time it was. Strange women approached Kenichi all the time. They seemed to think that he might be a cure for their loneliness.

"It's time for us to go home," I said, standing. Kenichi stumbled as he stood, and took hold of my arm.

I gestured towards the bar. "There's a clock over there."

WE WALKED TO OUR building. The sky was clear, and the air was crisp in that perfect autumn way.

"Why are you still in New York?" Kenichi's voice was steady. He sounded sober.

"I'm working on my screenplay."

"If it was done, would you stay?"

"Sometimes when I'm walking down the street, it still feels like I'm watching the city on TV."

"It's not home."

"No," I said. I had been in New York for over two years. I couldn't pass for a New Yorker, but to most people, I appeared to be an American from the west coast unless I said "about" or "sorry." In those days, I said *sorry* as often as I said *please* or *thank you*. I have since broken that Canadian habit of apologizing for minor mishaps such as accidentally brushing against someone on a crowded subway train, but my accent remains the same.

"So, why are you still here?"

"I need to finish the screenplay."

"You could write it from anywhere."

"I guess so. I like living here. Every day feels new and strange." In many ways, the United States remained a mystery to me despite a childhood informed with American television, movies and books. Although we had lived in New York for several years, Kenichi and I were unable to form an opinion about Americans or their culture. The only Americans with whom we had meaningful interactions came from a certain class. The Americans we knew had attended private schools and liberal arts colleges, if not Ivy League universities. Many spoke of summers at the Cape as if it were the only such land formation in the world. The future held promise for all of them; when they spoke of being broke, it was only a transitory state. For most, money loomed in their futures, whether through job prospects, inheritances or marriage. Once, while drinking overpriced cocktails at a bar not fancy enough to warrant the outrageous cost, a classmate spoke at length about how she "could not afford *anything*" because of tuition and I could not keep my eyes off her thirty-thousand-dollar engagement ring.

"Good night," said Kenichi in a sleepy tone.

"Night."

We parted ways.

The first time we met, we were standing in the lobby checking our respective mailboxes when he asked me if I was the tenant who watched Wong Kar-wai films late at night. I apologized ("I'm sorry") but he said, "Oh, no, I don't mind. I live in the apartment next to yours."

"Kingsley?" I asked, remembering the name on the intercom outside the building.

"Yes. My first name is Kenichi."

"Sophie," I said.

"Sophie, do you want to go see *2046*?"

"With you?" I said.

He ignored my question. "There's an advance screening tomorrow. I have two tickets."

We went. We were ambivalent about the movie, but we liked each other's company.

I ENTERED MY APARTMENT to find that my roommate, Sarah, was asleep. I tried to step softly past her room, but alcohol lent my gait an uncharacteristic heaviness. It didn't help that I was wearing heels and walking across a hardwood floor. Although I had been raised not to wear shoes indoors, I followed the customs of Sarah and my previous two roommates and kept my shoes in my bedroom. Rather than bathing at night, I bathed in the morning. I had made small changes to my personal habits so as not to irk my roommates even though New York was only a chapter in my personal narrative. I knew that one day, when I was no longer paying tuition, the United States would not want me within its borders and I would have to move on.

Ever since my grandmother died, I had been avoiding Sarah. She had what passed for happiness, and I did not want to impose on her because she was in the last stages of her dissertation. I was hardly ever home, and when I was it was usually past midnight. Sarah was a morning person. Our schedules did not mesh.

During the day I worked on my screenplay in the library. When I say work, I mean to say I watched films in the Butler Library Media Center and took copious notes. I was in possession of eleven medium-size black notebooks filled with pedestrian thoughts on hundreds of films. There was a notebook devoted to zombie movies, and another one on vampire flicks. I devoted two entire volumes on heists, trying to figure out just what made Le Cercle Rouge and The Taking of Pelham 123 so appealing to me. No genre was beneath my notice. Although I didn't believe that it was possible for me to fall in love, I watched romantic comedies. I knew that I would have a better chance of selling a love story than an action film because I was a woman. That was supposed to be my territory: shopping and grooming and courtship and marriage.

I was so lost during this time that I thought that seeking order and predictability would free me in some way. Therefore, the teen comedy My Boyfriend's Back merited the same careful attention as Ingmar Bergman's The Seventh Seal. I read movie reviews online and academic essays in obscure journals, believing I would find the formula for success. My compulsive research did not gain me exit from the hell that was writer's block. I began to hate opening Final Draft on my computer. The cursor on the blank screen seemed to mock me with its steady blink.

Aside from grief, during this period my other constant preoccupation was money. I had mounting student loans; my inability to finish writing the screenplay prevented my graduating in a timely manner. I wanted very much to finish. I devoted hours to sitting in quiet places, writing outlines for the second and third acts of my film. But as I sat in front of my computer, I felt like I was a failure. I would never be able to write anything worth watching. No one would ever want to buy my screenplay and turn it into a movie. This paralysis seemed too much to overcome.

When I was tired of working on my screenplay, I turned to odd jobs. This was against the terms of my student visa, but somehow it made me feel better. Each morning, I scanned job postings and emails in search of a few dollars. Although my great-grandfather had been a scholar, his fortune had been lost even before the Communist era and all the older men in my family were labourers. Writing did not seem a particularly honest way of earning a living. When I reported what I was doing to my parents, it sounded lazy. Who of their generation could believe that watching a film constituted real research? There were times when I thought I should have attended law school instead; I was an excellent reader and researcher, and I was relentless at completing tasks when I felt there was little at stake. Most nights I could not sleep thinking that my father could have retired early had I not decided to pursue my film school insanity. This only compounded my fears of failing to complete my screenplay.

KENICHI CALLED ME, BEGGING me to accompany him to a party a student from his cohort was hosting. "I don't want to go—but you know how it is," he said. "I have to make an appearance."

"Can't you go alone?" I could think of many things I'd rather do with my evening than attend a party thrown by one of Kenichi's acquaintances, such as defrost my refrigerator or alphabetize my DVD collection.

"I'll get you drunk before we go."

"Do you really want to have a drunk guest at a school function?"

"It's not really a school function. And since when have you been that kind of drunk girl? Besides, I'll behave better if you're there. Even when you're intoxicated, you're sensible."

"Come over with a bottle of Maker's Mark." I disliked many of Kenichi's cohort, but some of them amused me, like specimens in a freak show.

After four bourbons, we arrived at the party at 11:30. I was verging on belligerence. When I drank, I said cruel things about strangers and acquaintances, cutting remarks I would not utter while sober. Whether alcohol was a truth serum or demonic possession, I wasn't quite sure.

As we stepped into the living room, Jenna Kim—a girlfriend of an American named Chad or Chuck or Chandler who specialized in Joseon dynasty history and who directed all his conversation at my breasts whenever I had the bad luck of speaking with him—was sitting in a chair in the middle of the room. Her skirt was hiked up to her waist, and she wasn't wearing panties. She had a cigarette in one hand, and was blowing smoke out of her vagina. Jenna was famous for this at parties. She called it her "Singapore hooker trick."

"Oh, fuck, not again," I said loudly. "I need another drink." I went into the kitchen. Kenichi followed.

"Is this type of behaviour common at parties in North America?" he asked, amused.

"She's such a fucking moron," I said. "Singapore is the least likely Asian setting for this kind of desperate sex work. I mean, if she had said Thai hooker trick, I'd still be annoyed with her, but at least she wouldn't come across as so utterly stupid. She has no sense of political and socio-economic realities in different Asian countries. You'd think all of Asia was poor and backwards from her estimation of Singapore."

Kenichi laughed. "She's got a cigarette in her pussy and you're thinking about socio-economic factors and its influence on prosti-tution?"

"Whatever. I was saying that she's a stupid, self-hating, attention-seeking bitch. I bet she thinks she's a feminist. She probably writes poetry using feet binding as a metaphor for her dislike of her father, even though her family is Korean."

"Let's punish her by finishing off her soju." Kenichi held up a couple of green bottles.

"I bet Chad or Chuck or Chandler brought those," I said, reaching for one. "Cheers."

And so we drank away another night.

ONE DAY, JUST AS a chill had set in, I found a job posting asking for a Chinese speaker. Although it didn't specify a dialect, I knew they were seeking someone fluent in Mandarin. My abilities in standard Chinese were rather limited; I spoke Cantonese with my family. Since becoming depressed and broke, however, nothing shamed me and I no longer had qualms about telling untruths. I sent an email stating that I spoke Chinese. I received a phone message in Mandarin from someone named Kay asking me to meet at Dodge Hall that afternoon.

I walked across campus, passing Low Library. When it was warm out, the stairs leading up to the entrance was filled with people. But because it was cold, there were only a handful of students sitting down.

At Dodge Hall, there was only one Asian woman standing on the steps. I assumed this was Kay. "Hello," I said in Mandarin. "I'm Sophie. Are you Kay?"

"You're a Cantonese speaker," Kay said when she heard my accent.

"Yes," I said, switching back to English, not wanting to embarrass myself any further.

"You're in the film program," she said.

"How did you know that?"

"You're friends with Sam. You're in his films. I've seen all of them. Sam and I used to work together in Singapore."

"You're in the visual arts program."

Kay lit a cigarette. "And how did you know that?" She exhaled.

"I think it's your glasses," I said. "Actually, you were in my international student group for orientation last year. I was the peer mentor." Kay was one of the people I often saw in Dodge Hall whom I wanted to befriend, but had never figured out a graceful way to do so.

"I can't see without them."

"A blind artist," I joked.

"Colour and motion are okay. I don't photograph, and I don't do fine drawings or detailed paintings."

"Sculpture?"

"Installation, mostly. Some video." She peered at me closely. "How tall are you?"

"Five two."

"Hmm." She continued to stare at me.

"I think we're the same height," I said.

"Come by my studio." She handed me a card with her name and a telephone number embossed on it. "You know where the studios are, yes?"

"Prentis."

"Right." She put out her cigarette and left me standing on the stairs.

A FEW DAYS LATER, on my way back from grocery shopping at Fairway, I decided to stop by Kay's studio. I called her.

"Yes?" she said.

"It's Sophie. From the interview."

"I was wondering when you would call."

"I'm at Prentis, but I don't have swipe access to the building. Long story, but I keep losing my ID card. The guard is away."

"I'll be right down."

Kay opened the door for me. She was wearing what appeared to be layers of burlap.

"Isn't that itchy?" I asked.

"I'm wearing it over clothes," she said. "The burlap isn't touching my skin. It's a bit cold in my studio, and this was lying around."

As we walked up the stairs, I began to feel apprehensive. I had not yet seen her work, and I was worried I might not like it. Although it was irrational, if I didn't like someone's artistic output, I found it difficult to be civil. I was lucky to have friends that could abide my pretensions and neuroses.

When we entered her studio, I felt relieved. There was no evidence of mediocre work, only projects in progress that held promise.

"Would you like a drink?" Kay asked. "I have tea, coffee and scotch."

"I'll have a scotch," I said.

She handed me a generous glass of the liquor.

"Where are you from?" she asked.

"Vancouver," I said.

"I hear it's beautiful."

"In parts," I said. "I guess when I think about it, I focus on the areas that are picturesque, like the water and the mountains and the forests. But the city has an ugly side to it as well, like all other places in the world."

I walked over to a wall covered in photographs. "I thought you didn't take photographs."

"That's documentation of a performance I did last year. I don't photograph with the intention to show."

"They're good," I said.

"I didn't take them," Kay said, laughing. "I paid someone to document the piece for me."

I nodded to show that I understood, and took a sip of my drink.

"So, I guess you know that I don't speak Mandarin very well," I said.

"It's okay," she said. "There's no job. I wanted to see who would answer the ad. It's part of a project I'm working on."

I felt relieved that I wasn't going to be called on to be an interpreter.

"Your friend, Kenichi," Kay began.

"Oh, you know Kenichi?" I asked.

"We all know about Kenichi—all the women in my program, and some of the men, have tried to talk to him at some point," she said.

"But no one knows him. Except for you."

"He's my neighbour," I said.

"He's not your boyfriend?"

"We're just friends."

"How can you be just friends with him?" she asked. "Are you blind? I think you need to get your eyes checked. I'm not the only one with poor vision." She smiled.

"Are you interested in him?" I asked.

"No, he's not my type," she said. "But he seems to be yours."

"I don't know about that," I said.

THE NEXT WEEK, KENICHI's therapist upped the dosage on his medication. He called to cancel Thursday night drinks because he had slept through class and didn't intend on leaving his apartment.

"Why don't we go have dinner instead?" I said, concerned that he was slipping into a deeper depression. "If you haven't been outside all day, it might be good to get some air. Have you eaten?"

"I'm too tired," he said. Then he hung up.

I watched two movies and took notes. By midnight I was exhausted, but I couldn't sleep. I called Kay. I had discovered that I could always count on her to be awake at odd hours. Her studio didn't have windows, and she often lost track of time. As well, her schedule remained fixed to Singapore time despite the fact that she had lived in New York for over a year. I had never thought to question why she had not acclimated to Eastern Standard Time.

"Are you busy?" I asked.

"Come over," she said.

I was also privy to the knowledge that Kay was grieving, but she had never told me for whom. I was too polite to ask, and she was too private to talk about what was bothering her. Sometimes we sat in her studio drinking tea in silence. It was enough to know that someone else was going through the same thing.

"I'm worried about Kenichi," I said when I reached her studio.

"Why?"

I told her about his missing class, and cancelling our standing appointment. But then I began to talk about my inability to work, because that was also worrying me. I began to speak as if I were delivering a monologue.

"Perhaps I'm defeating myself," I said. "What is grief? It's just a transitory thing. I wish I could think myself out of all this and just write. It feels as if I'm using it as an excuse not to work."

I WAS DETERMINED TO start afresh. I scrapped the screenplay I had been working on and started on a new one, a romantic comedy. But every line I wrote seemed false. My protagonist was too much like me, too afraid to be vulnerable, too afraid to love.

Kenichi called. "Why are you like this?" he slurred.

"Like what?" I asked, curious.

"Nevermind," he said. "I need to go back to sleep."

"Good night," I said. When I hung up, I wrote our conversation into my screenplay.

THANKSGIVING CAME AND WENT. One morning I woke up at 8 A.M. and felt buoyant. I don't know what had changed, but something was different even though nothing had happened to warrant a change, except perhaps the passing of time. Maybe the day was particularly bright, or I was clear-headed for the first time in a long while, but there was a sense that I had attained a freedom of some sort.

Rather than plan my day around drinking, I made myself breakfast and sat down and wrote twenty pages. Later, I threw out those pages. There was nothing worth reading, but it was enough. I called Kenichi. I called Kay. I bought groceries and called Sarah to tell her that I was going to cook dinner, and that she should join me.

That night, the four of us ate together, telling funny stories about our childhoods and drinking two bottles of wine. Sarah went to bed early, and Kay had to return home to make a phone call to Singapore. Kenichi and I began walking to the bar we always went to on Thursday nights.

"Did you get a haircut?" Kenichi asked me as we walked down the stairs.

"No," I said.

"You look different," he said. "Better."

Out on Seminary Row, I had an overwhelming urge to hug Kenichi. I put my arms around him, and buried my face into his coat. He smelled so deliciously clean. He put his hands at the small of my back, and it felt as if he was holding me up, preventing me from sinking into the ground. Snow was falling, and gathering on our clothes. The tears I had been holding back for months came up like a tsunami, unstoppable. My grandmother was dead. But I was alive. I would live.

"I think this is what it's like to feel happy," I said.

Rerun

TODAY'S MY BIG DAY. I'm getting married. I should be happy, but there's this weird numb feeling in my chest that has nothing to do with the silicone bags shoved under my skin. The thing is, the groom is seventy. I'm twenty-four. The marriage was my mother's idea. She's planned my entire life from the moment of my adoption. She chose me from a Korean orphanage. This wedding is part of my comeback after a long stretch in rehab. I have a drinking problem. I destroyed my acting career because I liked drinking better than working. But I'm here now and I don't regret the past.

"Who says there are no second acts in American life?" Mom says. She's stabbing bobby pins in my hair. Drawing blood.

The man's children are all older than me. None of them are coming to the wedding. There's no pre-nup and they don't trust my intentions. They're right—what started all this was a problem with taxes. I hadn't been paying my fair share. Then the authorities caught on, so Mom devised a plan for me to catch a rich gentleman and get him to settle my debts for me.

The zipper on my dress is stuck.

"You've gotten fat. I told you not to eat the pasta last night."

We're at an impasse. I start thinking that maybe this is a sign I shouldn't get married. But this doesn't stop Mom. Nothing stops her. She tugs. The zipper gives way.

As I walk down the aisle, I marvel at the obscene floral arrangements. The bridesmaids all look like sausages encased in giant frills. I chose their dresses. I must be a misogynist.

The old man is standing there, waiting. He's a bit hunched over, and his skin is so saggy that he looks like he's a different species of animal. Sometimes he takes his teeth out before he kisses me. We haven't had sex. He thinks I'm a virgin, saving myself for marriage.

The thought of fucking him is what stops me. I'm halfway up the aisle when I turn around. The guests start to murmur.

"You," I say to a waiter. "I saw you arrive on a motorbike. Take me away from this."

"I'm working," he says.

"Give me your keys then."

"Why should I?"

The guests are rolling video and loving every second of this. I toss my bouquet to the ugliest girl in the crowd. Maybe her dreams will come true.

"Candy, get over here," Mom says. I ignore her.

I go up to the waiter's boss. "He's giving me a ride home," I say. She doesn't tell me no. No one tells me no, except Mom.

I take off my shoes and run to the bike. The waiter takes me to my house. He tells me his name is Jae, as if I care.

We end up in my bedroom.

"I used to masturbate to your TV show," he says.

I laugh. "Didn't everyone?"

"But I stopped."

"Why? Did your palms get hairy?" I take off my dress.

"Can you put your dress back on?"

"Don't like what you see?" I inch closer to him.

He steps away from me. "I started thinking that you might be my sister."

I pull my dress back on. The zipper gets stuck, but I'm mostly covered.

"I'm adopted from Korea too," he says.

It's clear we're not going to fuck. I flop down on my bed.

Jae sits down next to me, shoving a pillow between us. He turns on the TV. We watch a rerun of my show, *The Adoptees and Me*. I'm fourteen in the episode. A drugstore clerk catches my character shoplifting condoms and calls the police. My pretend parents are upset. Pretend me simpers and smirks and sobs and gets out of trouble.

"Your tits are still real this episode."

"They were real for the entire run of the show."

He smiles, revealing crooked teeth.

For some reason, I think we're going to be friends. I let him fall asleep on my bed. I'm sure he won't rape me. I don't think that incest is his thing. I stay up, waiting for Mom. She must be really mad at me, because she doesn't come home. I start worrying. I call my AA sponsor, Nikki, because even after a year of sobriety I find myself baffled as to how to handle this situation. After I monologue for ten minutes about how I know that one drink is too many, and that there isn't a thing I can do about yesterday, but due to this setback with my mom I feel I'm on the verge of returning to my drinking career, Nikki tells me I need to express myself in my own words. "Stop parroting the language of recovery literature," she tells me.

"I'm at my best when I follow a script," I say, because this is the truth. I learned how to be honest at AA meetings. At a young age I also learned that directors hate it when actors ad-lib.

I hang up. I can't have a drink and I don't know what else to do, so I stand at the window trying to find the Little Dipper and the North Star, but it's too smoggy to see anything clearly.

The next morning there's big news: my mother has gone and married the old man.

FOR THE FIRST WEEK after the wedding, I call Mom every hour I'm awake, but she never picks up. I doubt she still considers my taxes her problem. Or maybe she's on her honeymoon and doesn't have cell reception. I hope. I call my sponsor. We talk about my abandonment issues. I try not to slip into feelings of uselessness and self-pity. No matter what happens, I choose not to drink.

My accountant tells me to sell the house. I refuse. I can't imagine living anywhere else. Until I was nine, we moved at least once a year. We lived in some really gross places. What if I move and Mom comes back and can't find me?

"Maybe our real parents can help you out," Jae says when I tell him about my problems. Now that he's found me, his possible sister, he's determined to find his biological mom and dad.

"Maybe my pretend parents can help me out," I say, rolling my eyes.

"You should get a job," he says. His tone is sitcom tough love.

It's been more than a year and a half since I've worked. I thought I deserved a break so I fired my agent before I went to rehab. Acting is kind of lonely, really. I started drinking because I was so sick of pretending to be other people. Now that I'm sober I just want to be myself, but I really don't know who I am without Mom or my career.

I start looking for work, but it seems I am not qualified to do anything except be a stripper.

Jae intervenes. "Quit trying to solve your problems by taking off your clothes," he says. It might be the best advice that anyone has ever given me. I listen. He gets me an interview with his boss, Jill.

"I used to watch your TV show," Jill says.

"You remind me of my TV mom," I say.

"Why do you want this job?"

"I like paying my taxes."

"When can you start?"

"This week. But I can't work on Monday nights."

THE FIRST JOB IS a wake for a sixty-four-year-old man. His widow, Tiffany, is twenty-three. She's got massive boobs and an even bigger fortune. All the bachelors who approach to offer their condolences look like predators stalking prey.

"His children were older than their stepmother," Jill says. "What was he thinking?"

"Can't fault him for wanting the latest model," I say.

"Well, I wonder what she married him for. What?"

"I hear he was devastatingly funny and had a big dick."

A woman in an evening gown waves me over. I hold out a tray of wine to her.

"You're Candy Warner," she says. She's looking at my boobs, waiting for an answer. One of her eyes is bigger than the other and her veneers are too big for her mouth.

"I get that a lot," I say. "People also say I look like Lucy Liu, even though she's old."

She accepts a glass of wine. The look in her eyes tells me she doesn't believe me. I am not a very good actress. People around the room are whispering and pointing at me. I work hard at getting everyone drunk so that they'll forget they saw me.

LATER I GO OUTSIDE for a cigarette to escape the humiliation of it all. It's the one habit I just can't quit. Maybe it's because I started smoking when I was eleven, or maybe it's because it reminds me of Spencer Sparks, the guy who was my pretend older brother. We'd sit in his dressing room, smoke and play cards between scenes. My other pretend brother Jameson Cheung cheated at cards and was a sore loser. Jameson is in Hong Kong now, where he's so famous he can't walk down the street without being chased by little girls. He sends a lot of text messages about parties and hot chicks. Spencer is an A-list star. So I guess I'm the black sheep of our pretend family. I don't have any siblings in real life. Mom only had enough money to adopt one child.

Once outside, I discover I don't have a lighter on me.

"Do you have a light?" I ask Jae.

"This is like the episode where you sneak out of the middle school dance with the bad kids and the most popular boy in school peer pressures you into taking a drag off his cigarette," he says, handing me a lighter.

"It's just like that. Except I'm so much older and wiser."

"And your breasts were real then."

"Fuck off."

"I'm sorry," he says, putting a hand on my shoulder. I don't turn around.

"Come on," he says.

I ignore him.

"Stop treating this like a fucking soap opera," he says.

"I'm not. I never worked on a soap opera."

Jae laughs. We go inside to clean up. I find a champagne cork.

"Strange. Jill doesn't bring champagne for wakes," Jae says, holding up another cork.

We find a couple making out behind a curtained alcove. The man is not wearing pants. The woman is not wearing a shirt. We send them home.

Right before we leave, I go to the bathroom. When I open the door, Tiffany is standing in the door frame. I can smell gin on her. For some reason, I thought she'd be a vodka drinker.

She leans forward and slurs, "So Candy, I heard you like pussy."

"You're mistaken. I'm allergic to cats," I say.

Tiffany looks scared. She cries into my shoulder. "I'm all alone now."

I feel sorry for her. She doesn't even have a pretend family.

JAE GIVES ME A ride home. The thing is, I never learned how to drive. Mom was always around, or the studio would send a car.

When we reach my house, I say, "I think I'm going to quit."

"Quit?" Jae asks.

"It's humiliating being recognized."

"Being homeless is pretty humiliating too. But it's your life."

He leaves without saying goodbye.

I don't actually go through with quitting because the next day my accountant gets real on my ass about how I'll lose the house for sure if I don't work, so I decide to stick it out. I can't lose the house. There is nothing left to do but take responsibility and face my fears.

After I try calling Mom, I phone Jae to tell him I haven't quit. He offers to move in and pay rent. "We can search for our real parents together," he says. When he arrives at my place, two suitcases are all he has. I wonder if this is the new freedom and new happiness that I'm supposed to find in my sobriety.

Months go by. I call Mom every day. I leave messages for her. This is the longest I've ever gone without speaking to her. I know she's doing okay because she has a reality TV show with the old man where they go around the world visiting all the places they always wanted to see but couldn't because of their children. Jae tells me I shouldn't watch the show, but I can't help it. I watch a lot of TV because I'm afraid to go out to places where I might drink. I know I shouldn't do this, but sometimes my pride gets in the way and I can't just accept that I'm weak and it's okay.

Spencer calls to offer to get me a part in his next film. For a moment I think it might be nice to be paid a lot of money.

I tell him I already have work.

"That's great," he says. "What are you working on?"

"Oh, I guess you might say it's a comedy. You might say it's real life."

MY DAYS ARE A blur. Wake, wake, wake, wake, christening, wake, wake, wake, wake, sweet sixteen, wake, wake, engagement party, wake, wake. Then it's a flurry of weddings. I start hoping for a wake to break the monotony of true love and gold-digging. Finally, someone dies.

"This is like the episode where your great-uncle dies and everyone at his wake is a mortician," Jae says.

I hold a tray of red wine out to a man who is talking to a woman with a bad nose job.

"I'm king of plots," he says.

"Oh yeah?" the woman says. "What do you do?"

"I sell burial space."

I sigh. At least he isn't a wannabe screenwriter.

At the end of the night, as Jill and I are loading the van, I say, "That was my 250th wake."

Jill gives me a strange look. "That was a retirement party."

WHEN I GET HOME, I listen to my cellphone voicemails. None of the messages are from Mom.

There's a message from my former agent, Camilla.

"Candy, your twenty-fifth birthday is coming up! Don't think I've forgotten. By the way, *Playboy* called. Do you still like long walks on the beach and watching the sunset with your boyfriend? You haven't gone and found religion, have you? Stop sabotaging yourself and call me."

I remember Jae's advice and resist the offer.

I call Mom. I want to tell her that I've turned a corner. I'm no longer afraid of economic instability. I might even believe in a higher power. She doesn't pick up so I leave another message.

A FEW WEEKS LATER, Jae and I are about to go to work a wake when he gets mail.

"We're not related after all," he says, handing me an official-looking letter.

"You've been as good a pretend brother as my other pretend brothers have been. Maybe even better," I say.

We celebrate with orange juice mixed with soda water. At least, I celebrate because I have very unsisterly feelings towards Jae. It's a relief that my thoughts are no longer possibly incestuous.

We go to an enormous house for the wake. It looks very familiar, like I've seen it on TV. I'm circulating with a tray when I see the old man I was supposed to marry. I search the room, but I don't see Mom.

"Where is my mother?" I ask the old man.

He blinks at me.

"Is she here?"

"She's dead," he says.

"Dead?"

"This is her wake."

"She can't be dead," I say. "I just left her a voicemail this morning."

Jill tells me she'll pay me for the shift, but I should stop working. Someone hands me a glass of wine. I take a sip and immediately spit it out. I sit on a couch and stare at all the strangers. Who are these people?

Soon, most of the guests are gone. I remain to help clean up.

"You don't need to stay. You should go home," Jill says. She sounds every bit like my sitcom mom.

"I'm not ready to leave yet," I say.

I've had a lot of practice pretending to be sad, but I've never experienced real tragedy. I'm off script. I don't know what to do. I find myself baffled. Is this the work of a higher power? Is this the grand plan for my life? Before I descend to self-pity, Jae takes me home.

I tell Jae I just want to be alone. He understands, and goes up to his room. I go out into the backyard for my last cigarette of the day. The moon is bright. The air is cool. I can hear my neighbour's music: "Candy Says," by the Velvet Underground. Sometimes when I was little, Mom would play that record for me. For a moment, it's like we're back in our first apartment, before we started moving around and before I started acting. In the distance, a woman laughs. I take a deep breath and try to think of nothing.

Jae recently cleared the flowerbed of dead plants. I remove my shirt and skirt and lie down upon the earth. My body sinks into the cold ground. I think about how I didn't even get to see the casket or the burial. I light another cigarette. Inside the house, the phone is ringing. Is it a journalist? A telemarketer? The only thing I'm sure of is that it won't be Mom. Pretend or real, I am no one's daughter now. I stare at the sky for a long time, and succeed at last in locating the North Star.

The Boy Next Door

EACH MORNING, AFTER GETTING dressed, Kent Lee took a photograph of the view outside his bedroom window. He began the practice at age eleven when he received his first camera, a birthday present from his parents. Thirteen years later, he was in possession of over four thousand photographs. He rarely looked at the images, choosing instead to focus on the future. He had a five-year plan. One day, once he became an art director at a glossy magazine he'd be ready for marriage, most likely to his current girlfriend, Jessica, whom he had met at university on the first day of class. Perhaps they would move from Vancouver to Toronto, where his parents lived, and buy a house. He would no longer live in a basement suite that faintly smelled of mildew.

The morning of Friday, October 1, 1999 was uneventful. The sky was overcast. When he later developed the film containing the day's snapshot, the photograph was ordinary—it betrayed no sign that anything was amiss. But that afternoon at work, the managing editor asked to speak with him privately. Once they were seated in a meeting room, she informed him that the magazine was restructuring and that he was being laid off. If he wished, he could provide his services on a freelance basis.

KENT FEARED TELLING JESSICA the news. To begin with, she hadn't approved of his career path. She was in her final year of law school, and when she wasn't in class or studying, she waited tables, determined not to accrue debt. He admired her determination; he felt it was one of her best qualities, and it made up for his own deficiencies.

He kept his unemployment a secret over the weekend. They ran errands, went to the beach, watched a movie and had sex. On Monday morning, he woke up and put on his office clothes as though he were going to work. He paused at his bedroom window, but didn't take a photograph. Once Jessica left for class, he gathered some CDs he hadn't listened to in months and biked to Zulu Records.

A clerk he had met at an Evaporators show, Alex, was working.

"What's new?" Kent asked.

"Have you heard the new Magnetic Fields? *69 Love Songs,*" Alex said.

"I lost my job."

"That sucks."

"I have some CDs to sell." Kent handed Alex a pile of albums.

"Cash or credit?"

"Cash."

"Are you going to the Gaze show?" Alex passed him twenty dollars.

"Maybe," Kent said, though he meant no because he didn't want to spend money on a ticket.

He left the store and biked to the employment insurance office to apply for benefits. Then he bought a bottle of white wine for Jessica using some of the CD money.

At home, he prepared dinner while listening to a Shellac record, *Terraform.* Jessica returned at six o'clock, and the food was ready. He waited until she was finished her second glass of Sauvignon Blanc before confessing that he was no longer employed.

"Oh," Jessica said.

"I qualify for employment insurance," he said. "I applied today."

"This is an opportunity for you to change careers," she said. "My cousin Mark told me that his bank is hiring. I can give him a call."

"That's not part of the plan," he said.

"I'm not hungry," she said, pushing her plate towards him. "Thank you for cooking." She took her wineglass, walked to the living room and turned on the TV. He heard the theme music for *Friends*, a program that she loved and he loathed.

He sat by himself at the kitchen table, and finished her portion of chickpea stew and brown rice.

KENT PRETENDED TO BE asleep while Jessica got ready for class. As soon as she left, he put the Smog album *Red Apple Falls* on the stereo and read *Punk Planet* for half an hour before getting out of bed. Unemployment, he decided, was akin to a vacation. He was determined to enjoy his time off.

After searching through the cupboards for food, he settled down to watch *Passions*, a soap opera so ridiculous that it was transfixing. He flipped through a book of photographs by Garry Winogrand, and thought about taking pictures of people hanging out on Main Street. The hours slipped by, and by five o'clock he was bored. He looked in the fridge and saw the unfinished bottle of Sauvignon Blanc next to eight rolls of film. It had been six years since he'd had alcohol of any sort—he had been straight edge since the summer before university started. He stared into the fridge for a minute before deciding to have a glass of wine. Then he had another.

Jessica returned home to find him on the couch, drunk. "I guess you've outgrown your straight-edge phase," she said. "What's for dinner?"

"Leftovers. We should finish the chickpea stew before it goes bad," he said.

"Can you do the grocery shopping tomorrow? I'm meeting with my study group in the afternoon, but I'll be back in time for dinner."

"Sure."

"How was your day?"

"I have an idea for a new photo project."

"Mark said you should give him a call. Maybe we can have brunch with him on Sunday. He has some leads for you."

Kent took in a deep breath. He didn't want to fight with Jessica, so he said, "Thanks."

"Do you mind if I study while we eat? I'm a bit behind in one of my classes."

"Go ahead."

He read a newspaper while she highlighted a textbook. His stomach didn't feel quite right, and his head was starting to ache. By 10 P.M. he was ready for bed. He put the dishes in the sink, and resolved to wash them first thing in the morning. Jessica remained at the kitchen table with her books.

WHEN KENT WOKE UP, he discovered that Jessica had already left for school. His body felt dry, and he had a headache. He glanced at the Garry Winogrand book on the nightstand and thought about taking photographs.

In the kitchen, he saw that the dishes were done. He washed down an Aspirin with a cup of coffee. Shortly after, he threw up in the bathroom sink.

Halfway to Main Street, he realized he didn't have his camera with him, so he decided to go grocery shopping. The liquor store beckoned, so he bought a bottle of wine, a six-pack of beer and a bottle of whisky.

He returned home in time to watch *Passions*. Partway through the episode, the telephone rang. He picked it up on the third ring. It was Jessica.

"You'll have to eat without me. I'm covering for Heather at the restaurant—the bus is here. Bye!" She hung up.

Kent did not enjoy eating alone, so he had a bowl of instant noodles, drank four beers and fell asleep on the couch.

Hours later, he awoke to find that Jessica had placed a blanket over him. It was still light out. Or was it another day?

The couch was comfortable, and soon he was asleep again.

ON SUNDAY MORNING, JESSICA tried her best to rouse Kent from bed.

"We're having brunch with Mark and his wife," she said. "Get up!"

"I think I have the flu," he said.

She gave him a look that indicated she didn't believe that he was ill, but half an hour later she left without him.

He stayed in bed.

When he next saw Jessica, her first words to him were, "Are you going to look for work today?"

"Of course," he said, pulling the duvet over his head as she closed the door and left for school.

Twenty minutes elapsed. He couldn't get back to sleep, so he rose and went into the kitchen.

The table was covered in paper, bills mostly: telephone, credit card, hydro, student loan, another telephone bill. There was a calculator, a pencil and a notepad next to the open envelopes. He could see that Jessica was worried about money. It was time for him to find a job.

He turned on his laptop and searched the Human Resources Development Canada website, applying for jobs ranging from dishwasher to photographer's assistant. Then he scanned through the newspaper and spent the afternoon composing cover letters and tailoring his resumé for each posting.

JESSICA RETURNED AT MIDNIGHT to find Kent watching television.

"I'm sick of this shit," she said, pushing the papers from the kitchen table onto the floor. "I hate my job." She pushed her bangs from her eyes, and he could see that she was crying.

He walked over to her and massaged her shoulders. She relaxed a bit. He kissed her neck and unbuttoned her blouse. She pushed his hands away.

"No sex until you get a job," she said, and made him sleep on the couch.

KENT WOKE UP WITH an erection. He'd been dreaming of Jessica. He started to masturbate, but he began to think about money and work and failure. Why hadn't anyone called him for an interview? He let go of his cock and reached for the telephone. There was no dial tone. The phone was dead.

He got off the couch and turned up the heat. He looked out the window at the phone booth on the corner. It was raining. He sighed, and put Cat Power's *Moon Pix* on the stereo. After drinking a cup of coffee and eating a piece of toast, he took four quarters from the laundry jar, which was nearly empty, and went outside.

First, he called his brother Ron. "Can I use your pager number on my resumé?"

Ron said yes.

There were three quarters left. Kent looked at his list and ranked the jobs in order of desirability: the most appealing was a photographer's assistant position. A phone call later, he had an interview scheduled for the next day.

RAIN FELL AS KENT rode his bike to the interview. He was listening to Destroyer's *City of Daughters* on his Discman. His brown polyester pants were soaked. As he approached his destination, the smell of death filled the air. The office was near a meat-processing factory, and the stench of rotting flesh permeated everything. He locked up his bike, then gagged and dry heaved, steadying himself on a graffiti-covered brick wall. There was a sticker that read OBEY GIANT.

He entered the office through an unmarked door. A woman wearing a headset sat at a large table, reading *Cosmopolitan*.

He walked up to her. "Hello, I have an interview. My name…"

She looked up from the magazine and gave him a surly look. "Wait over there." Kent tried to smile at her, but she was focused on reading. He backed away and looked past her into the hallway. There was a watering can, a chair and a milk crate.

"Carl," the woman said into her headset. "Your three o'clock is here."

Kent noticed that his pants were dry and pondered the miracle of polyester.

"Go down the hall," the woman said to Kent. "It's the blue door on your left."

As he walked to Carl's office, a blonde woman in a white terry cloth bathrobe passed by. She looked Kent up and down and licked her lips. Kent kept walking until he found the blue door.

The office contained a table, two chairs, a computer and a phone. Carl was a large man with massive arms. His chest was twice the breadth of Kent's, and he was wearing a ring with a huge diamond on his left pinkie. He didn't look like any of the photographers Kent knew.

"I didn't think you'd be Chinese," Carl said, gesturing to a chair. "I'm not sure you'd be the right fit. Now if you were a girl that would be a different story."

"I don't follow," Kent said, sitting down.

"I'm just telling it like it is. How old are you, sonny?"

"Twenty-four," Kent replied, staring at Carl's mouse pad. It bore a picture of a naked, red-haired woman with her legs spread open. She had a Brazilian wax.

"You like that, I can tell," Carl said, pointing at the mouse pad. "That's great. So, can I see some ID?"

Kent took his driver's licence out.

After examining it carefully, Carl said, "Good, good. Legal. I don't want any trouble."

There was something about Carl that Kent found distasteful, but he wasn't sure what it was. He pushed the thought from his mind, concentrating on how happy Jessica would be if he found employment.

"So you think the job's easy, do you, sonny?" Carl asked.

"I've done it before."

"You have?" Carl raised an eyebrow. "In Vancouver?"

"Yes."

Carl's gaze drifted to Kent's crotch. "Sonny, just cause you fuck your girlfriend doesn't mean you can do this. You gotta fuck in front of people with the cameras rolling. You think your erection can handle that?"

"What?"

Carl held his hand up to indicate that he wanted to finish speaking. "This isn't like fucking your girlfriend. Can you get erect on cue?

Cause we're not going to baby you. This isn't a fucking sperm bank. We gotta put you through some tests. Have you masturbate in front of the camera guy..."

"I think I'm in the wrong interview," Kent said in a loud voice.

Carl sat back and stared at Kent. "Shit, sorry." He paused for a moment. "You sure you don't want to give this a try?"

Kent was about to say no, but Carl named a sum equivalent to his share of the rent for a day's work. He thought of Jessica studying with her law school classmates, and he knew that she would slip away from him if he didn't take action.

A minute later, he found himself reclined on a bed, pants and underwear around his ankles and cock in his hand. Carl and a camera guy were watching him. He thought of Jessica, but he couldn't imagine her naked, not with a hot light shining upon him. He tried to think about the first time he saw her in his bed. Nothing worked. He couldn't get hard, even though he hadn't had sex in weeks.

"For fuck's sake, we haven't got all day," Carl shouted.

Kent thought of the unpaid hydro bill. He wondered how much more disappointment Jessica could handle before she decided to leave him. "I'm trying," he said, pumping his cock faster. But it was no use. He wasn't accustomed to being naked in front of other men.

"You can stop," Carl said.

Kent thought about how dark it would be when the electricity was cut off. "Please, give me another minute," he pleaded.

"It's not going to happen," Carl said.

Bile rose up in Kent's throat. He pulled up his pants and started to walk to the exit.

Carl grabbed his arm, shouting, "Where are you going? This is Winston, the camera guy." Winston stepped out from behind the camera. Kent wondered if he had been filming, and a cold feeling took hold in his chest.

"This is Kent," Carl said. "He wants to be your assistant."

"Hello!" Winston said, extending his hand for a shake as if he had not just witnessed Kent's humiliation.

"Step into my office." Winston led Kent across the room.

As Carl left he shouted, "Don't smoke in the studio!"

"Yeah, yeah. You tight-assed bastard," Winston muttered. "You'd think he was running a baby food company, the way he goes on about shit." He turned to Kent and lit a cigarette. "This is our little secret. Sit down." He pointed to a couch. It was a set prop. Kent hesitated, then sat on the edge of a cushion and tried not to think about how the couch was used.

The half of the room they were sitting in was a replica of a living room. The other half was a dominatrix dungeon fashioned like a cave. In addition to medieval stocks and wrist restraints on the wall, there were metal cylinders, chains with clamps, chains without clamps, and whips and dildos in various sizes.

"It's not a hard job. It doesn't fucking matter. You're just pointing the camera at pussy. The only rule is: you can't fuck the girls. If you want to fuck the girls, you do it in front of the camera. Do you understand?" He blew smoke in Kent's face. Kent felt ill; his feet were asleep and a sheen of cold sweat covered his body. Winston continued talking.

"My last assistant forced girls to service him. He fucked the girls, I fired him. It's sexual harassment to fuck the girls, so don't be poking your dick in their pussies or any other holes. That's fucking harassment."

Kent eyed the door. It wasn't far—ten steps at most. He could get up and run for it. Winston wasn't as intimidating as Carl, and he probably wasn't much of a runner.

Winston continued. "Like I said, the job's easy. The thing is, when people are having sex for long periods of time, it gets messy. You'll get to hold the camera after a while, but you'll also be in charge of the mop and bucket."

Kent tried not to dry heave. He shifted closer to the edge of the couch, wondering if they ever cleaned the covers.

"So, can you start this week?"

"I'm still a student," Kent lied.

"What are you studying?"

"History."

"I fucking love fucking history. You gotta remember though, on this job, you can't fuck the girls."

"I'm a full-time student," Kent said. "I have to go to school every day."

"Oh," Winston said, putting out his cigarette. "Too bad. You seem like a nice kid. You probably wouldn't have fucked the girls."

KENT BIKED QUICKLY TO escape the stench of meat. The rain had stopped, and he dodged a number of puddles as he rode through the streets. Fugazi's *Steady Diet of Nothing* was blasting through his headphones. Halfway home, the smell of smoke enveloped him, but he continued to pedal.

Just up the street, a house was on fire. Flames were shooting into the air, sparks threatening to ignite the homes next door as well as the tall tree in the front yard. He dismounted, unable to ride by without stopping to look. He marvelled at the jagged flames. It was the biggest fire he'd ever seen. It was out of control.

Several other people were standing on the sidewalk, watching the house burn. One woman was crying. For the first time since losing his job, he took his camera out and started shooting. *Click.* The windows shattered. *Click.* Fire trucks pulled up. *Click.* The roof on the next house caught fire. *Click.*

When he finished the roll, he turned his back on the house. He got on his bike and pedalled hard. His hair and clothes smelled of smoke, and rain began to fall. He wanted to get home before Jessica did. He wanted to develop the roll of film so he would have something to show her, an accomplishment. To make her smile again—could he hope for more? The streets flew by: Victoria, Fraser, Main. He had thought that happiness had been eluding him, and existed only in the distant past or in an unattainable future, but as he cycled home, he knew he was wrong.

Left and Leaving

IN THE WINTER OF 1997, world leaders descended upon Vancouver to discuss important matters. Two kids in Victoria battered and drowned a girl they barely knew. The dead girl, Reena Virk, and I were the same age: fourteen. Dozens of women who lived in the Downtown Eastside had disappeared, but few people seemed concerned. I was preoccupied with my own troubles. My older sister, Lisa, could not stay sober to save us having to move from one foster home to another. Our mother continued to be missing. In my imagination, she was merely out of town.

"She'll be home for Christmas," I said one afternoon. Lisa and I were sitting in a wooded area behind the high school we were attending that month. She was smoking a joint. The wound over her right eyebrow, a gash acquired from falling down a flight of stairs during a fight at our last school, had closed with the help of five stitches. There was going to be a lasting scar, one so prominent that it altered her appearance. I wondered if her father—we had different fathers— would recognize her if they had a chance encounter on the street.

"Mom's probably dead, you know," Lisa said. She started laughing. I couldn't tell whether it was the pot or if she was just callous.

"Shut up," I said. I had many thoughts about our mother—some horrible—but I didn't want to believe she was dead.

Lisa and I were living with foster parents, Edward and Judith Forsythe, because we had run out of family. I worried we would soon run out of fosters. People Lisa and I lived with either left or died. In the span of three years we'd passed through the care of our mother, my paternal grandmother, a great aunt and an uncle who was the younger brother of Lisa's father.

Neither Lisa nor I recalled our fathers. Mine was half-Chinese, half-English. Hers was Haida or Coast Salish—we weren't sure which. There was little family resemblance between us. I was short and had pale skin and black hair. Lisa was two years older and eight inches taller than me. This never stopped her from borrowing my clothes—everything in my wardrobe was slightly too big for me. Her skin was several shades darker, while her hair was several shades lighter. She resembled our mother more than I did, which had made me very jealous when we were still living with Mom. Lisa and I took turns being the beauty of the family; it wasn't hard to share because there was only one other person to divide things with.

I liked living with Grandma best. We ate dinner together every night and she taught me how to bake cookies and cakes. The radio was always on if we were in the kitchen. I'd dance around with flour on my hands and ask to see pictures of my father when he was a boy.

Mom used to call Grandma's from time to time, and when the phone rang I would run to get it. Every call was the same: I would ask if she was going to come back, and she would promise to see us soon. But it was all promises and never the real thing.

During one particularly cold winter, Grandma fell down the steps in front of her house and broke her hip. Her health declined. After she died, Lisa and I moved in with our great aunt Mary. Mom stopped calling. I liked to think it was because she detested Mary. Later, when we lived with Lisa's uncle Will, Mom still didn't call. Now that we were with the Forsythes—strangers—it seemed possible that our mother would never find us again.

We had been living with Edward and Judith for a few months. I figured either they were really nice, or they didn't know any better. I could imagine living with them for a long time. Their house smelled like laundry and flowers. Mom's apartment never smelled like that. It held an odour of whisky and beer and cigarette smoke. That was Lisa's scent. I wondered if it was mine as well. For the longest time I had wished we were twins. We would have the same mom and dad, and maybe they would have stayed together.

THE SUN WAS DISAPPEARING into the water and the sky was pink in spots. It was growing darker, and colder.

"We should go back to the Forsythes," I said. I didn't want to be late for dinner and dessert. I was also hoping to rummage through their fridge and well-stocked cupboards.

"I've got plans," said Lisa, looking past me.

"Oh," I said, trying to make eye contact, hoping for an invitation. Lisa wouldn't look at me. There was a silence that seemed to last an ice age. Lisa didn't tell me where she was going and we parted at the SkyTrain. I returned to Edward and Judith's alone.

The Forsythes lived a few blocks from Kits Beach. They had a twenty-year-old daughter named Jun who was at McGill studying anthropology. Edward and Judith adopted Jun from South Korea. Jun called them "Dad" and "Mom."

When I got to the house no one was home. There was a free weekly paper sitting on the table next to the door, unread. I picked it up and went into the kitchen to grab a bag of chips and a big glass of water. Edward and Judith didn't eat junk food, but kept chips and cookies and pop and candy on hand for us. Sometimes, if I was sitting in their kitchen or listening to the radio, I imagined myself back at Grandma's.

I entered the living room and sank onto the couch. The coffee table was the perfect size and height for reading a newspaper. I turned the pages with my left hand and shoved chips into my mouth with my right hand.

The newspaper had only bad things to report. Photos of missing women accompanied the headlines. The stories were about women who hadn't made it home in a long time. The missing women left a legacy of abandoned journals and uncashed checks. All of them lived in the Downtown Eastside and were poor. I wondered why the authorities were acting as if twenty women had just wandered off, and would reappear at any time.

Every day I looked at different newspapers to see if my mother was ever front-page news. Although she never appeared, I noticed that a lot of the women reported missing looked like her. I wondered if any of them were from the same nation. I didn't know much about my mother's ancestry; she never got around to teaching me about her parents or her grandparents. I didn't know if they went whale hunting or lived in longhouses or wore cedar hats. I learned about traditions that may have belonged to my ancestors during social studies every year. Lisa told me that everyone, including the teacher, always asked her about potlatches and button blankets and the Haida artist Bill Reid, but she didn't know. She didn't have any answers for them.

I FELL ASLEEP ON the couch and woke to the sounds of cooking: metal clinking against glass, the sizzling of water and oil, and Judith singing songs from *The Sound of Music*.

"Rough day at school?" asked Edward, who often said things that were unfunny, but he was so well meaning that it didn't matter. I liked the predictability of his personality. He was dependable, constant down to the knot in his tie and the polish of his shoes.

"Yeah," I said. "We're playing football in PE."

"I hated gym," said Edward.

"I don't like it very much, either." I got up. "I should set the table." I gathered up my glass and the chip bag and entered the kitchen. "Hello, Judith."

"Hello, Annie. How was school today?"

"Good."

"Learn anything interesting?"

That morning my locker partner, Kelly, told me she was pregnant.

"Charles Dickens was paid by the word," I offered. "We're reading *Great Expectations*." I didn't add that I'd finished the book a week ago. I read during lunch because I had no friends at school.

"You should read *Jane Eyre* when you're done."

"I've read it before." We chatted about orphans as I set the table for four, even though I wasn't sure if Lisa was going to make it in time for dinner.

Judith was lifting the pot of green curry from the stove when Lisa came through the back door.

"Smells good," Lisa said. "Anything I can do to help?" She reeked of pot, but neither Edward nor Judith said anything, though they gave each other looks that could only be interpreted as knowing. We sat down to dinner as if we were a family.

ACCORDING TO OUR MOTHER, Lisa's dad was a drinking man. Those were mom's exact words. She said it as if he were an *athletic man* or a *renaissance man.*

"He was a good man when he wasn't drinking," Mom would insist and I would stare at her left leg, which was shorter because she had broken it three times. Three separate accidents.

"Too bad he was never sober," Lisa would say, as if she remembered. But she'd never even met him. He was gone before I was born and became the excuse for everything that had went wrong in our lives.

"My father was a drunk," Lisa would say whenever a teacher caught her drinking or if she hadn't done her homework.

Once, when the lunch monitor caught me smoking on school grounds I said, "My sister's father was a drunk." At the time, I didn't know enough about my own father to use him as an excuse.

THE NEXT DAY, I got to school well before the bell rang. My promptness had a lot to do with the fact I'd left the house without Lisa, who was still sleeping as I packed my school bag. I shook her, but she swatted at my hand and told me to leave her the fuck alone.

At lunch I went out onto the school's front lawn. Lisa was on the sidewalk waiting for me.

"Let's go," she said.

I had PE and home ec. in the afternoon, so I agreed even though I had reservations about skipping classes two days in a row.

We got on a bus, and as we passed Chinatown Lisa pulled the ringer and insisted that we eat egg sandwiches at one of the Hong Kong cafés that Grandma used to frequent.

After we ate, we decided to walk to Gastown. When we got to the

Woodward's building, which had been empty for four years, there was a group of people standing on the sidewalk. Each person was holding up a piece of paper. At first, I thought they were advertising cheap pizza or drink specials at some nearby bar. But there was urgency, not boredom, in their eyes.

"Have you seen this woman?" a man asked, thrusting a piece of paper at me. It was a missing poster printed on thin stock. The woman pictured looked older than her twenty-two years.

"No," I said.

A woman approached Lisa with a poster of a different woman.

"I know her," Lisa said.

The latest woman to disappear used to live in Uncle Will's building. Her name was Diane. She used to stand on the street and scream then buzz our apartment because she'd lost her keys. Sometimes men would knock on our apartment door, thinking it was hers. I learned every sort of insult a man could shout at a woman from the things these men would say while kicking on our door.

A woman named Martha told us she was Diane's sister, and held up a picture from the past. None of the images looked like Diane. The girl in the pictures didn't have dark circles under her eyes. That girl was smiling. Even when Diane wasn't crying, she didn't smile. Still, I took a poster to put over the desk in the bedroom Lisa and I shared.

"They'll never find her with that picture," Lisa said to me as we walked to Edward and Judith's.

"Maybe she's not missing. Maybe they just don't recognize her," I said.

Lisa looked at me as if I were the stupidest person alive.

THAT NIGHT WE WENT to a party in an abandoned house. Lisa got really drunk. The party ended when some kid overdosed and his friend called the paramedics, who were accompanied by two cops. Lisa and I ran for a few blocks to a bus stop. After waiting for twenty minutes, we decided to walk home because it seemed the buses had stopped running for the night.

A few blocks from the Forsythes' place, she stopped and threw up into her hands.

"Why didn't you just throw up on the ground?" I asked as she wiped her hands on her jeans, which she had borrowed from me.

"Whatever."

"Are you okay?" I asked.

"I'm fine."

"Then hurry up. It's almost 2:30."

Ten minutes later we walked into the Forsythes' living room to find Judith asleep on the couch and Edward watching an infomercial about a muscle-stimulating machine.

"You should have been home two hours ago," Edward said. His tone was calm. In our three months in the Forsythe household neither he nor Judith had raised their voices. The quiet reminded me of living with Grandma.

"Sorry," I said. "Lisa's not feeling well."

"I'm feeling just fine," Lisa said. She lay down on the floor. "I'm just fine. I can take care of myself."

"I'm sorry," I said. Edward nodded and helped carry Lisa up to the room she and I shared.

"I love you," Lisa said to me, and closed her eyes. She started snoring.

"How was the party?" Edward asked as we tucked Lisa into her bed.

"It was boring," I said.

"Sounds like the party Judith and I went to tonight," he said.

"I doubt it."

"You still want to go the movies on Sunday?" Edward asked.

"Yeah."

He closed the door softly, as if he was afraid he'd wake Lisa up. It had only been three months, after all. He probably hadn't noticed that Lisa could sleep through anything: thunder, earthquakes, neighbours screaming at each other.

EDWARD MADE GOOD ON his promise and took us to the movies. Judith, who was a nurse, got called into work so we went without her.

"I want to go downtown," said Lisa.

"Can we go to the Woodward's building first?" I asked. Edward said yes to our requests, though he probably thought mine was strange.

We were excited about the movies, but Lisa and I wanted to see if Martha and the other people we'd seen holding the missing women posters were still around.

When we got downtown, we discovered that Martha wasn't in front of the Woodward's building. There were other people holding flyers for their missing sisters, daughters and friends.

"Would you stand out here for me?" Lisa asked me as I collected posters to take home.

"I'm here with you now," I said.

A FEW DAYS LATER, I waited for Lisa at her locker after my last class. Thirty minutes went by. Finally, the vice-principal walked past and stopped when she saw me.

"Annie, Lisa was sent home early today. She's been suspended."

I didn't ask why.

Lisa was already at Edward and Judith's by the time I got there. I stared at her black eyes and fat lower lip. She was drinking iced tea through a straw while watching a talk show. Two young women were running at each other, screaming. The television audience cheered.

"I broke a boy's nose," she said when she saw that I was looking at her.

"Why?"

"He was talking shit." She didn't elaborate further.

At our last school, Lisa lasted only six weeks before getting expelled. She accomplished that by getting into three fights. I had been hopeful that she had stopped fighting at our new school.

I went upstairs to pack my suitcase, anticipating that we'd be asked to leave.

EDWARD AND JUDITH CARRIED on as if Lisa hadn't been suspended. Lisa didn't get into any more fights, but she still stumbled home drunk from time to time. And she had taken to smoking pot on the back steps of the house. "Don't shit where you eat," I said to her, but she didn't listen to me.

After a while I thought about unpacking. Lisa hadn't sparked any new violent incidents at school and I was tired of wearing the same clothes over and over again. After dinner one night, Edward and Judith asked me to sit with them in the living room.

Judith wouldn't look at me, so Edward did all the talking.

"We want to adopt you," Edward said.

This was rather unexpected. They were really the nicest and most patient people I had ever met. "Lisa will be so happy," I said, because they were waiting for me to say something.

Judith still wouldn't look at me.

"Annie, we want to adopt *you*," Edward repeated.

"Oh," I said. "Oh. No."

I ran upstairs. Lisa was lying in bed, drunk and crying.

"I'm not going to leave you," I said, hugging her. She continued to sob, and I didn't know what to do. I started to laugh, and then the laughter became tears. Finally, we both fell asleep.

IN THE MORNING THE window in our bedroom was wide open. Lisa's clothes were still hanging in the closet and heaped on the floor, but mine were gone.

There was a note pinned under Diane's "Missing" poster: "Sorry I took your clothes."

O, Woe Is Me

THERE ARE SIX OF us sardined into the trailer behind the empty lot, which is strewn with mismatched furniture covered in violent paint splotches. Our boss, Artie, refers to the lot as "our money maker." The rest of us call it "the pen" or "the shooting gallery." I like to think of it as "the office," because it's where I spend most of my work hours.

We are congratulating our soon-to-be-former colleague Mark on his new career, one with possibilities of fame and fortune: competitive eating. Tomorrow he will no longer be one of us, a freak. His trips to Coney Island will be limited to Independence Day, when Nathan's has its annual hot dog–eating competition. When he has a family, he might even take them to the beach or boardwalk. But he's not the kind of guy who would let his kids play our game, Whoop the Freak. Mark's not cruel.

"To Mark, the best employee I've ever had," says Artie, raising his hot dog. He pauses, not used to giving compliments. "May you eat and eat and never explode."

We all raise our hot dogs, too. In response, Mark stuffs his hot dog—bun and all—in his mouth and seems to swallow without chewing. I take a small bite of mine and chew slowly, wishing Artie had sprung for beer. Then I slap Mark on the back and say, "I hope you beat Kobayashi." Everyone laughs, because they think that I look like Kobayashi. The only things that Kobayashi and I have in common are that we have Japanese parents and we are men.

Joe, who has three young children and works the dreaded morning shift says, "Do it for America, buddy."

Mark eats ten hot dogs without breaking a sweat. He eats the way he works: methodical and relentless. I've only seen him eat ice cream and dumplings in events sanctioned by the International Federation of Competitive Eating. Last year, when he was runner-up to Takeru Kobayashi in Nathan's Fourth of July hot dog–eating contest—the glamour event, the figure skating of competitive eating really—I was dodging paintballs in the Whoop the Freak pen. After his second-place finish, he did a lap on the boardwalk with our nation's flag draped over his shoulders. I saw him jog by and couldn't help but be jealous. I had harboured dreams of swallowing cannoli whole ever since I had to give up my pro ball dreams.

"Twenty, twenty, twenty!" The other guys are shouting so loud that tourists have gathered around the trailer. A boy perched on his father's shoulders is rolling balls of snot on one of the windows. It's Tuesday—my day on cleaning duty—so it'll be me out there with newspapers and Windex polishing the glass until Artie can see his reflection in it.

Mark eats his twentieth hot dog as if it were his first. I cheer, but I'm thinking of other things.

My cellphone beeps. It's a text message from my girlfriend, Melissa: WHERE R U, LOSER?

MARK AND I GREW up together in Bensonhurst. Back then he was a skinny kid who read comic books and couldn't catch a ball to save his hide from beatings. So I exercised my power as wide receiver and track and field star to keep him intact at school.

I'd say, "He's cool. Leave him alone." The guys would back off, but the best part was the girls. Suzy or Laura or Tiffany or Amber would say, "Oh, Yoshi, that was so sweet," and later tell me in private that her parents were out of town.

I had it all then. My father thought I'd be a sports star and my mother dreamed I'd be a neurosurgeon. Sometimes I wonder what might have been if Suzy hadn't been drunk on prom night and hadn't pressed her car keys into my clammy right palm on account of the fact that I didn't drink then. I had an athletic career to think about, full-ride offers from three colleges.

Mark was the first person on the scene. He was riding his bike (having skipped prom) and when he saw the carnage he sprinted like a Tour de France cyclist to a payphone.

When I am not feeling depressed I tell myself that Suzy had so much beer that night she was probably in a happy state when the truck struck her dad's little brown car and killed her. Other times— most times—I line up all the bottles of pills from the medicine cabinet on the bathroom counter and think about how I cheated death even though I'm a lousy card player and even worse at chess.

I came out of the accident with a broken leg. The colleges withdrew their offers and I continued to live with my parents while classmates moved away.

Enter Melissa. When we met she played the Smallest Woman in the World in the carnival freak show. She's not really the smallest woman in the world, just an actress/bartender. The trick involved costumes and mirrors. To my great disappointment, I learned that most freak show attractions have an element of fakery. Above all, I was crushed to discover that the bearded lady was really a man. Anyhow, all those illusions deluded Melissa into thinking that her pity for me was love. At present, her feelings are likely closer to disdain.

Now Mark is heading to the finish line and I'm a fool looking over my shoulder. I'm John Landy and Mark is Roger Bannister, passing me by.

THERE'S A NOTE ON the kitchen table from Melissa when I get back to our apartment.

We're out of toilet paper.

No *Love, M* or little *x*'s and *o*'s. Mel used to write affectionate missives. She used to put on too much lipstick and kiss me on the forehead while I was sleeping. She once had pet names for me that I liked. Now I'm just *loser* or *jerk*. I can't remember the last time she touched me voluntarily.

Melissa and I keep missing each other. When I think of our

relationship, there's a pit in my stomach, the same feeling I used to have if I knew I was going to drop the ball. I don't want to fumble us. So I buy some toilet paper, family size and not just four-rolls-for-a-buck, and wait for her to come home.

I MAKE THE MISTAKE of closing my eyes for a few minutes. Hours go by. When I wake up there's a new note on the kitchen table:
   Audition today. At work tonight.
   No hearts, not even a thank you. This does not bode well. In high school I was good at three things: running, catching a ball and getting the girls. I can still run and catch, and at the moment I'm not concerned about getting the girls. Keeping one girl, that's the hard part. I'm sure that Melissa is slipping through my fingers.

BESIDES MELISSA, ALL I have is my job and that's not much. After high school I discovered that I wasn't even cut out to operate deep fryers. I have no marketable skills other than my ability to run and catch. I can't swallow swords or breathe fire so I ended up becoming one of four guys who dodges paintballs and rotting vegetables for a living. A new breed of Coney Island freak.
   Whoop the Freak is the brainchild of Artie Daniels, former car salesman. Artie was walking down the boardwalk when he noticed the game Shoot the Freak and decided he wanted in on the action. Whoop the Freak has a smart business model. The overhead is low. The pen is filled with furniture Artie found on the sidewalk. Other than paying a few guys to be freaks, he only has to maintain a small trailer, the five paintball guns mounted at boardwalk level and a couple of slingshot/mini-catapults. To make Whoop the Freak slightly different from Shoot the Freak, Artie accepts rotting produce from various grocery stores and has a "Rotten Tomatoes" option where people can choose to sling putrid fruits and vegetables at fellow humans.
   "Paintball's bullshit," he told me during my interview. "People don't want to be shot at. They want to be the shooter. That's where

you come in. You're the shootee, the freak. The rotting produce provides a historical touch to our endeavour, which is more than you can say for Shoot the Freak. If you're good, it'll be like Shakespeare."

At the start of every shift I think, *To be or not to be?*

NOW THAT MARK'S ONTO greener pastures, the other guys and I have our eyes on the lucrative weekend days. So far Artie hasn't scheduled anyone for Saturday or Sunday. Nor has he mentioned whether or not he's going to hire someone new.

"The element of surprise and money are the only reasons to get out of bed," he often says when someone asks about schedules or their future with Whoop the Freak.

I get to work early to make sure that the windows on the trailer are clean. They are, but the trailer is covered in graffiti. There's an anarchy symbol next to PETER LOVES CAITLIN. There's also a crude approximation of a naked woman.

Artie keeps a can of white paint on hand for this very reason. I slap on the first coat in ten minutes, but it does little to hide the damage. As I wait for the paint to dry, I wonder if I'm showing enough initiative to take on Mark's old workload. I marvel at my new brown-nosing self.

When I see Artie the first words out of my mouth are, "So who's working the weekend?"

He points to a button on the lapel of his sports jacket, which reads, ASK ME TOMORROW.

At least he didn't point to the one that says, WHAT'S YOUR PROBLEM, FUCKFACE?

Then he says, "Let Joe finish the trailer. You're on."

So I suit up. Shin guards, body armour, bulletproof vest, motorcycle helmet. I walk to the pen and sit on the sofa. All the items in the pen are supposed to represent items you might find in someone's living room. Well, items you'd find in a freak's living room. Behind the living room set-up is a picture of a stage with red curtains painted on an old billboard. Everything is covered in paint or rotten food and there's nothing private about the space. The boardwalk overlooks the pen and there are usually about forty people standing around listening to Artie's spiel and staring at the freak.

My favourite thing about my workspace is the dirty white refrigerator, which sits next to the dirt patch that becomes a mud pit when it rains. The fridge looks a lot like the one in the apartment I grew up in, except my mother always kept ours fully stocked. It isn't plugged into anything and even if it were, it probably wouldn't work. I keep my empty beer cans in it. Some entrepreneurial soul empties it out every night, saving me the trouble.

After the fridge, I'd have to say that I like the sofa, mostly because it is good for hiding behind. I have no real use for the broken office chair, except that it is a convenient place to put an ashtray. The reason why there is an ashtray is Artie felt that I wasn't treating the workspace with respect.

"Would you drop cigarette butts on the floor of an insurance office?" he barked on my first day on the job.

"I guess not," I said, but I wasn't sure. I'd never set foot inside an insurance office. All the insurance people I've ever met showed up to see me at the hospital after the accident.

I take the helmet off and light a cigarette. Up above, Artie's firing up the crowd.

"There are no prizes here, no stuffed animals. If you're looking for that, go somewhere else. If you're here to Whoop the Freak, you came to the right place. Five shots, three dollars. That applies to the rotten tomatoes as well."

No takers yet.

I think about Mark and competitive eating. I think about how I thought I could out-eat everyone until I heard that Kobayashi ate fifty hot dogs. When I saw a picture of him—he's a little guy—I quit. I don't like losing and losing to a little guy is not an option.

And now I am here, sitting between two buildings, waiting to be shot.

The first shooter of the day is a five-year-old boy. I see the mother putting three bucks in Artie's hand. She beams at her child. The little boy gets me in the stomach before I've had a chance to put my helmet on. I start running between the sofa and the refrigerator.

Another paintball flies towards me and I dive behind the office chair, knocking the ashtray off. Then I sit on the chair and spin around and around.

The mother gives Artie another three bucks. On his last shot, the little boy gets me right in the chest. I start an elaborate death sequence, clutching at the spot where I think my heart is.

I say, "O, woe is me."

I drop to my knees.

"I am dead!" I collapse on my left side. All those acting classes. I count to ten before rising to my feet. When I stand, the mother throws a zucchini at my face and her little son cheers. I fall down again and close my eyes.

When I open my eyes, the boy and his mother are gone, but Melissa is standing on the boardwalk. She has a new haircut and I think that maybe her hair is a shade or two lighter. She looks pretty, but tired. Although Artie is not one to refuse money, he won't take the twenty dollars she's waving in his face.

"I don't get involved in my freak's personal life," I can hear him saying.

"Fine," she says and walks to the paint gun in the middle, stuffing her money in the back pocket of her worn jeans. She pulls the trigger and the first shot misses my helmet by inches.

"Is that you, Yoshi?" she shouts.

I don't say anything. Freaks don't talk directly to shooters.

She continues shooting. Then she uses a slingshot to launch a withered eggplant at me. "Aren't you going to ask how my audition was?"

A paintball hits my leg. Rancid apples fly past me. I say nothing.

A two-hundred-pound guy in a leather jacket tries to give Artie a twenty to join in the action. Artie says, "In a moment. Why don't you enjoy the free show for now?" Leather jacket nods.

I do a cartwheel. The paintball gun makes its release noise and paint flies towards me. I feel a sting on my left thigh. A bed of limp lettuce breaks my fall.

"Say something!" Melissa is using her stage shouting voice. Then she gets me in the chest. My heart tightens.

"Say something, you fool!" shouts a prim-looking woman wearing the kind of hat my grandmother might wear to church if she were still alive.

I drop to my knees and take my helmet off. I look up at Melissa, standing there on the boardwalk. Instead of collapsing and pretending to die I stay on my knees. I am Yoshihiro. No more rehearsed lines, no more thoughts of death. No finish line in sight, just starting blocks and the tension before the pistol goes off.

There is no script to follow. I know that now.

I say, "Will you marry me?" The women standing on the boardwalk start clapping and I imagine that Melissa's trigger finger is relaxed. The smell of paint and rotting food hangs around me. I stay on my knees and wait.

Little Miss International Goodwill

MORE THAN ANYTHING IN the world, eight-year-old Clementine Wong wanted to be blonde when she grew up. At Chinese school, when she was supposed to be memorizing characters for dictation, she drew pencil crayon self-portraits depicting herself as Rapunzel, Smurfette or Barbie. She was certain she would undergo a metamorphosis at puberty: her straight, black hair would soften into blonde curls like those of Amy March, who looked very pretty on the cover of *Little Women*.

Her secondary desire was to get the attention of her older sister, Constance, who never wanted to play. To achieve this, Clementine stood in front of the television while Constance studied a VHS tape of the 1988 Miss Hong Kong pageant. Constance believed she was destined to be Miss Hong Kong—or at least Miss Photogenic. She walked around the house with a book on her head to perfect her posture and did aerobics while listening to Leslie Cheung albums on the family's only cassette tape player.

"Move!" Constance said. She was watching reigning Miss Hong Kong and Miss Chinese International Michelle Reis's swimsuit interview, mimicking the beauty queen's mannerisms.

"No. I like it here." Clementine put her hands on her hips.

"Move, dummy."

"I was in the living room first," Clementine said.

"I was in the living room first yesterday," Constance countered.

"I was in the living room first last week."

"I was born before you, so I was in the living room first. Take that, second best," Constance hissed.

Clementine didn't know what to say, so she repeated herself. "I was here first."

"Mom!" Constance shouted.

Clementine didn't want to get in trouble, so she sat down on the floor to the left of the television, and picked up a Nancy Drew book she had borrowed from the public library.

Their mother entered the living room.

Constance smiled. "*The good part's coming up,*" she said in perfect Cantonese.

Clementine pretended to read for a few minutes while her mom sat with Constance, then she retired to her room to play with dolls. She had one Barbie, and she liked to make-believe that the doll was a baseball player or detective or explorer. Constance also had a Barbie, but she had converted the doll into Miss Hong Kong, complete with sash and tiara. She had even coloured the doll's hair with her mom's dark brown hair dye. This year the doll's name was Michelle. It changed from pageant to pageant, taking on the names of winners. Clementine's doll was called Barbie, "Because that's her name."

Each day, Clementine brushed the doll's blonde hair one hundred times. She'd read in a book that it was the magic number required for a perfect mane. When she was done, she brushed her own hair, and counted each stroke with her eyes closed as if she was playing hide and seek. At the end of one hundred strokes, she would open her eyes and look in the mirror. She was always disappointed that her hair remained black.

DURING DINNER, CLEMENTINE PLAYED with a hole in the elbow of her Expo 86 sweatshirt, a gift from an aunt who had visited Vancouver the year of the world's fair. Constance was sitting next to her. Her back was straight, and the hem of her dress fell neatly over her knees, which she held tightly together.

"You're still holding your chopsticks wrong, dummy," Constance said.

"I'm not. See, I can pick anything up." Clementine picked up a piece of beef and stuck it in her mouth. She chewed it with gusto.

"It's wrong. You're stupid because you weren't born in Hong Kong. You were born in Vancouver. You're a stupid *banana*. You speak Cantonese with a *banana* accent." Constance spoke softly so that their parents couldn't hear what she was saying.

"Shut up, jerkface!" Clementine shouted, slamming her chopsticks on the table.

Their parents heard that.

"Don't talk like that to your older sister," their mom said in Cantonese.

"I'm sorry," Clementine replied in English, though she didn't feel that she was in the wrong. When her parents weren't watching, she showed Constance a mouthful of chewed greens and beef.

"Mom! Look!" Constance said.

Clementine shut her mouth. She tried very hard to hold her chopsticks correctly so her parents would love her as much as they loved Constance.

THE GIRLS AT SCHOOL didn't like playing with Clementine. She roughhoused like a boy and didn't like to talk about clothes or horses. Sometimes she liked to sit inside for the entire lunch hour and read a book rather than play with other children.

"What are you doing?" Amanda asked her one rainy afternoon.

"Reading," Clementine said.

"Reading what?" Chantal asked.

"A book," Clementine said. She disliked Amanda and Chantal, who both liked animals, princesses and the colour pink.

"I bet it's hard to read," Amanda said.

"Not really. It's pretty easy," Clementine said.

"My dad says Chinese people have squinty eyes," Amanda said. "It makes it hard for you to see."

"Your eyes are weird," Chantal said.

"At least I don't have glasses," Clementine said.

"At least I don't have glasses," Chantal mimicked, though she was wearing glasses.

"You do have glasses, Four Eyes," Clementine said.

"But at least she's not ugly," Amanda said.

"And I'm not Chinese," Chantal added.

"I'm Canadian," Clementine said.

"My dad says you're not," Amanda said.

Clementine ignored her.

The next day during recess, she filled Amanda and Chantal's coat pockets with dirt and worms.

ALTHOUGH SHE WASN'T A good student, Clementine loved Chinese school. Classes were held in a school cafeteria, with one teacher in charge of students whose ages ranged from five to sixteen. The best lessons featured stories about young boys and girls who grew up to be great people. All the children attending the class aspired to greatness in some form: beauty queen, professional baseball player, medical doctor, war hero.

During break, Clementine listened to the older girls talk in the washroom about hair, makeup and boys. She thought that boys were gross, but the conversations were fascinating. Even Constance, with all her big sister knowledge, didn't know as much as Karen and Alice.

"I was thinking about bleaching the front of my hair," Karen said, staring at her reflection in a dirty mirror.

"Blonde?" Alice asked.

Clementine listened with interest.

"Maybe. I don't know," Karen said. She caught Clementine looking at her in the mirror.

"You should wear your bangs like this," Karen said, sweeping Clementine's hair to the left.

Clementine touched her hair. A feeling of happiness spread through her body. She now knew what it took to become blonde.

THE HOUSEHOLD BLEACH WAS in the laundry room, under the sink. Clementine shook the bottle. It was nearly full. She undid the cap and discovered that it smelled like motel towels and sheets. First, she tried to comb the liquid through her hair, but it was too difficult and most of it ended up on the floor. After some thought, she stopped the sink and filled it with bleach, then stuck her head in. A tingling sensation spread across her scalp. Quickly, it became uncomfortable.

Clementine stood up and started crying. Why did trying to be blonde hurt so much? A moment later, her mom walked into the laundry room.

"*What's wrong?*" her mom asked. She glanced at the telltale sink. "*Did you put bleach in your hair?*"

"Yes."

Clementine's mother led her to the bathroom and placed her head under the bathtub tap. As cool water dulled the burning sensation, her mom told the story of Fa Mok Lan, the brave girl who pretended to be a boy so that she could take her father's place in the army.

"Can I do that?" Clementine asked.

"*You can do whatever your heart wants.*"

When the water stopped running, Clementine sat up and looked at her mom. The light in the bathroom was strong, making her mother look very bright. The sting of bleach had worn off and the tub was nearly drained. As water dripped from her hair onto the floor, she remembered that when she was four years old she thought her mother was the most beautiful woman in the world. Her mom wrapped a towel around her head, gently drying her hair. Clementine closed her eyes. She hoped she would look like her mother when she grew up.

Robot by the River

I

WHEN I WAS TWENTY-TWO years old, I moved into a four-storey historic building in Vancouver called the Shaughnessy Lodge. It was the first time I'd lived on my own, without family or roommates, and at the time I thought of myself as brave.

I lived on the third floor in a bachelor. All the modern conveniences of the previous century were at my disposal: an icebox, where I kept my important papers; a Murphy bed, which retracted into a large cabinet with glass doors; a free-standing bathtub; and a compartment next to the door for milk deliveries. The windows faced an alley filled with garbage bins and cars. In the summer the smell of rotting food rose up, forcing me to decide between stale or fetid air in my small apartment.

The floors were hardwood, and I had to sweep weekly to prevent the accumulation of dust-and-hair tumbleweeds. When I chose to leave the safety of my suite, I'd take the stairs. The elevator was a wooden-panelled affair, but because the cables squeaked I was afraid to ride it. I thought the alarming noise was an omen. There was a Denny's within walking distance as well as a gas station, a Mac's Convenience Store, several car dealerships, three unimpressive sushi joints, a bike shop and a computer store.

That was also the summer my boyfriend Yoichi moved to London to attend graduate school in art history. He wanted to be a curator, and this was the first step in his plan for the future; he was the sort of person who finished every project he began. I tried not to dwell on his absence.

A tall, thin boy occupied the apartment above mine. He was so slight I was sure he was a vegan, even though he was as likely to wear brown leather Wallabees as Chucks. There was an air of distance in his demeanour, as if his body was present but his spirit was located eight thousand kilometres away in another country. It struck me that he was suffering some sort of deep sadness. I'm not sure why I thought this. Perhaps it was his posture or the tense fashion in which he held his hands that gave him away. When we passed each other on the stairs or in front of the building, he would say hello to me. His manner made it clear that he acted out of politeness rather than interest. I would always wait for his greeting before offering salutations of my own.

The first time I ran into him, I hadn't slept for four days because of a July heat wave. Everyone in the city was irritable, tired and sticky—it didn't help that transit workers were on a long strike. By the eighth of July there had been no bus service for one hundred days. I was on my way to see some bands from Vancouver and Victoria play at Ms. T's Cabaret; he was returning home, accompanied by a young woman with blonde hair and blunt bangs that rested just above her groomed eyebrows. The girl clutched his arm as if he was the latest handbag; she displayed the confidence of someone who was accustomed to being the most beautiful person in any social situation. Our three voices sounded mechanical in the stairwell: *Hello. Hello. Hello.* Later that week I encountered her on her own, and she walked past me without a word or a look.

During this time I subsisted on a string of odd jobs and freelance assignments. I was an office temp, proofreader, babysitter, tutor, DJ and web content editor. The theoretical knowledge I had acquired during my four years of studying communications at Simon Fraser University was rarely put to use by my numerous employers. Often, my temp jobs reminded me of high school: I felt bored, apathetic and lonely, and there was a touch of misanthropy in all my dealings with co-workers.

Yoichi and I agreed I would join him in London when I had saved enough money. My goal was twenty-five hundred dollars. The exchange rate between the dollar and the pound at that time was poor, and I didn't want to be broke in an unfamiliar city. Rather than taking on another job, or getting one very good job, I elected to cut costs by skipping meals, riding my bike and trimming my own hair. (When I look back at pictures of myself from this period, the word that comes to mind is *forlorn*.) Aside from rent and the phone bill, and the occasional pack of cigarettes, my expenses rarely exceeded forty dollars a week. But from time to time, I would meet a friend for a drink, which would turn into four or five drinks. One morning, after a night consuming gin and tonics on an empty stomach, I realized it was possible I would never save enough money to leave Vancouver for London.

THE FIRST TIME I saw the tall, thin boy away from the vicinity of our building was while I was working. The receptionist at one of the local weeklies was on vacation, and I was her replacement for six days.

On my third day of answering phones and signing for packages, the boy got off the elevator carrying a tripod and a large bag. Even though the leaves were just beginning to change colour, he was wearing a thick sweater and a coat.

"Hello," he said. There was a look of recognition in his eyes and since we had never exchanged names, I reached out my hand and said, "Hi. I'm Julia."

"I'm Oliver," he said. "I live in your building."

"I know," I said.

He asked to pick up a cheque. "My last name is Andrews." A pause. "I'm a Korean adoptee," he said, as if I had queried the dissonance between his surname and his appearance.

I asked him if the homeless man who sang opera while searching the back-alley Dumpsters for pop cans and bottles had woken him that morning. The man stopped behind the Shaughnessy at least once a week and had an impressive repertoire of French, German and Italian arias.

"I sleep through everything," Oliver said. "Even when you're listening to music late at night and Natalie can't sleep."

"Oh, sorry." I didn't know what else to say, so I started flipping through the cash box for the envelope with his name on it.

"It's okay. I like drifting off to your music," he said. "I've been meaning to pick up the latest Songs: Ohia album, but I don't need to because you have it."

If we had been in a high school TV show, he might have said, *My band is playing tonight. If you don't already have plans I'll put you on the guest list.* But since we weren't twentysomething actors trying to pass as lovesick teenagers, I gave him his cheque and he left.

THAT NIGHT, YOICHI CALLED me. He wanted me to send one of his books.

"I think it's in the box under your bed," he said. "The one marked THEORY."

"Will you be coming home for Christmas?" I asked.

"My parents want me in Halifax." A silence. "And I can't afford to fly to Vancouver as well. They're paying for my flight."

A plane ticket to Halifax was more expensive than one to London. I couldn't even suggest meeting him; besides, he had not extended an invitation. We had nine provinces and a frigid body of water separating us, and it seemed like the distance was widening. I began to doubt that a mere airplane ride could bring us back together.

A FEW WEEKS LATER, when the trees were bare and the sidewalks were covered in clumps of wet leaves, I ran into Oliver opening a new pack of cigarettes outside Mac's.

I told him about a job I interviewed for that hadn't panned out; a friend told me that the manager decided not to hire me because I'd given the impression that I wouldn't report to work on time. "Do you think it's because I don't wear a watch or because I was late for the interview?" I asked.

Oliver was lighting his cigarette, so he shook his head instead of speaking.

"Can I have one of those?" I said.

He tipped the pack in my direction. "Want to go for a drink?"

I said yes, and soon we were walking along Hemlock towards downtown. As we approached the Granville Street Bridge, the sun was beginning to set and the glass on the new apartment buildings in Yaletown reflected the pink light. The air was cool, not cold, making the walk pleasant. I began to think it was the sort of night where everything feels original and new, even the most clichéd thoughts and emotions. The sound of traffic on the bridge hid the fact that neither of us had anything to say at that moment. I wondered if he and Natalie had long conversations, or if she did most of the talking, or if they were silent most of the time. We passed the sign that read LIMITED VISION and the bridge curved ever so slightly. In a few minutes we were downtown.

We had our first drink at the Sugar Refinery. A band was just finishing with sound check, so if we wanted to stay longer we would have to pay cover. I had no desire to listen to live music that night or talk over a band's set, so we headed for Subeez. I hadn't eaten dinner, so I ordered some fries and a vodka tonic. Oliver was on his third drink and I was on my fourth when Kara Collins came to the table. Kara was Yoichi's friend from university—an artist whose primary medium was video—and I had met her at various parties and openings and shows.

"Hello," she said, kissing me on the cheek. "I haven't seen you in ages. Who's this?"

"Kara, Oliver," I said, trying my best to sound sober and in control.

"Nice to meet you," she said, and Oliver nodded. "How's Yoichi?"

"He's doing well," I said, even though I didn't know if that was true. He hadn't called me for two weeks, and every time I tried telephoning him I got his answering machine. "He may be coming to Vancouver in December," I added, though it was a lie.

"Oh, really? I thought he was going to be in Halifax," Kara said. "That's what he said in his last email."

I didn't know what to say. My face was flushed, and it became clear to me that I was quite drunk. How was I supposed to respond?

"I liked your show at the Or," Oliver said, coming to my rescue. "Especially the piece set in your studio."

"Thank you," Kara said, perking up. There was nothing she liked more than talking about herself and the excellence of her art. "I'm working on another piece at the moment. I was thinking a lot about Rodney Graham's work when I was shooting. Anyhow, I'm editing it right now. If you'd like, you can come over and view it when it's done." She leaned in a little, touching a pin on the lapel of Oliver's shirt. "Love this."

Oliver was looking a little uncomfortable now.

"So, Kara, have you and Michael found a new place yet?" I asked, regaining my composure.

"We're moving into a little place in Strathcona," she said, her eyes still on Oliver. "You'll have to come to our housewarming." As an afterthought she said, "Both of you."

She kissed me on the cheek again, chastised me for not calling her more often, and went back to her table.

"Want another?" Oliver asked, touching my glass.

"Yes," I said. "Yes, please."

||

THAT YEAR, IT SEEMED to rain all of November. I hardly left the apartment, except to go to work. I took up knitting. Although I was careful, at the end of each row I'd find that I had dropped a stitch or two. When I finished a scarf, which I hoped to give to Yoichi to wear when we met again in London, I unravelled the whole thing and started over, hoping I could get through at least once without missing stitches. I wanted it to be perfect.

Around me, relationships I had counted on as being till death do us part had begun to come undone like the scarf I couldn't finish. My mother was divorcing my stepfather, whom she had married when I was five. She called me every other day, and he called me weekly. I listened and told them both I loved them over and over again. My friends Stephen and Marie were also dissolving their marriage. Theirs was the first non-familial wedding I had ever attended. He wanted a child; she, another man.

My conversations with Yoichi were becoming shorter and shorter. Soon, all our words would be reduced to the length of an epitaph. I was having trouble remembering the lovely things about him, like the way he said my name or how his hands were always warm while mine were cold. And if I was having trouble remembering in the city where we had shared all our adventures, what was there in London to remind him of me?

When I felt I was spending too much time in my apartment, I went to concerts alone. At various venues, I ran into friends and acquaintances, but I was so unhappy that I had trouble sustaining conversation. After shows I ambled home, still wide awake. I listened to *Red Apple Falls* repeatedly, as if Bill Callahan's voice would some-how alleviate my pain. "Ex-Con" became my theme song; I was adrift in Vancouver, a robot by the river. I watched *Hard Boiled*, *Happy Together*, *Chungking Express* and *An Autumn's Tale* until I fell asleep. The days began to blur, and I longed to have a real conversation with someone.

Yoichi hated it when I smoked in bed, so I took every opportun-ity to do so in his absence. I'd be on the phone with him, puffing away. I said things like, "I'm tired of talking about Derrida. I'm so over theory." He'd get frustrated with my sweeping statements, and I would try hard not to cry while he was still on the phone.

I couldn't figure out where we were on the narrative arc: middle or end?

ONE WINTER DAY, WHEN the birds had migrated south and the roads were slippery with ice, there was a knock at my door. I wondered if it was my neighbour Jordan complaining about the noise level. He thought my way of cooking, bathing and cleaning was too loud. The sound, he claimed, prevented him from being able to draw and paint; he used his apartment as a studio. Most times he banged on the wall, but on occasion he was angry enough to come to my door.

"You're the most distracting neighbour I've ever had. How often do you have to bathe? I can hear you splashing in there," he told me the first time we met. He said this as soon as I opened the door, before introducing himself as the man who lived next door. "I can't work with you going on like that."

But it wasn't Jordan at the door. It was Oliver. He looked paler than usual and the bags under his eyes were more pronounced.

"Natalie's gone."

I had just read three novels by Haruki Murakami and for a moment I thought she had vanished, but then realized what he meant.

"Come in," I said, not knowing what else to say.

Oliver walked in and lay down on my kitchen floor. I stood next to him, wondering if I should let him know that I hadn't mopped in weeks. There was a stray Cheerio next to his ear, but he didn't notice. He was quiet for a moment, but then he began to weep. Prior to that, the only male I'd ever seen cry was my brother, and I had caused the tears. I didn't know what to do about Oliver. Perhaps other women have a sense of how to act in such situations, but I didn't have that gift. So I put the kettle on. I was naive and thought tea could make anything better.

When Oliver stopped crying, I handed him a mug. He sat up to take it. "The leaves are from my stepfather's garden in the Okanagan. Only there's no longer a garden, because he and my mom sold the house because they're getting a divorce." I said all of this as if Oliver hadn't been crying.

"I'm sorry," he said.

"I didn't even get to go home one last time."

"What was it like?"

"There were all these cedar trees in the yard. I used to lie in the grass and read for hours and hours. My bedroom was really small, but it didn't matter because there was so much space around."

We sat in silence for a bit. I got up and put a record on the turntable.

"Natalie likes coffee," Oliver said. "She's afraid to drink tea, especially if it's made with loose leaves and they get stuck to the bottom of the cup. She's not big on knowing the future."

I nodded, as if I understood. But most days I thought of nothing but the future. I dreamed only of positive outcomes, and I clung to the belief that things could only improve with time.

"We met two years ago at a party. It was a birthday party," Oliver continued. "We didn't get on at first. I was quite drunk and she was standoffish—she told me later that I reminded her of one of her ex-boyfriends."

Oliver continued to talk. It was as if he could speak freely now and before he could not. His tears washed away a barrier between us.

"I don't know how to be without her," he said.

"I understand," I said. "I'm trying to learn how to like being by myself. It's hard. Now that I've gone through all this, I'm not even sure if I should move to London. Would I be any happier there? Can being with Yoichi make everything right again?"

"You won't know unless you go."

"I guess so."

I noticed that one of the buttons on Oliver's shirt was about to come off. I took a safety pin from the glass cabinet and pinned the button in place. Everything about Oliver indicated that he needed someone to take care of him. This we had in common. Yoichi took care of me when we lived together: he planned and cooked our meals, and he paid our bills on time. I wondered what he was doing at that moment, if he had met a London girl in his building. The idea made me feel ill, even though it was only in my imagination.

I let Oliver sit on my floor and talk until dawn. Had it been later in the year, birds would have begun their morning song before the first light. He mostly spoke about Natalie—he was delivering a eulogy, gaining closure—but he also talked about his childhood on a farm in Manitoba and the years he spent homeless after dropping out of high school.

When Oliver ceased to speak, I told him about a show I went to earlier that week and how I was thinking about taking guitar lessons. He offered to teach me, and I accepted.

"You're the only person I've talked to for more than thirty minutes in weeks," I said. "Thanks."

Then we started laughing about an odd experience he'd had on a photo shoot that day. There was a harmony to our voices, which was soon accompanied by the sound of Jordan banging on the wall, imploring us to quiet down. For the first time in months my small suite in the Shaughnessy felt like home.

III

DECEMBER AND JANUARY SEEMED a blur of frost and discontent. Rather than make the trip to Kelowna to visit my mother—who was living alone for the first time in her adult life—I stayed in Vancouver to earn double pay during the statutory holidays. Saving money had become a habit, despite the fact I no longer wished to travel. I had not yet developed a taste for expensive things, so my bank account continued to grow at a steady pace. On Boxing Day, the temperature dropped to four below, and I stayed at work after my shift ended at a temporary retail job to enjoy the free heat and to avoid telephone calls at my apartment.

To my surprise, Yoichi was angry when I told him I would not join him in London. I had assumed he didn't really miss me all that much—I was mistaken. He told me that he would come back to Vancouver in June with the intention of staying for three months before returning to school and he asked me what I thought about that. I said I wasn't sure, and that I needed time to consider this new development.

"Is this because of that guy?" he asked. His tone of voice was aggressive.

"What guy?" I asked, mystified.

"Kara said you went to her housewarming party with some guy named Oliver Andrews."

I sighed. "We didn't go together. I saw him there."

"She said you *left* with him. Who is he?"

"My upstairs neighbour. You know, the tall Korean dude. He drove me home."

"I don't remember him."

"This isn't about him. I made the decision to stay in Vancouver for myself."

"Why don't you want to come to London?"

"What would I do there?"

"The same things you do now, only with me."

Yoichi continued to talk, but I didn't feel like listening. Our conversation was about to go in circles.

I hung up the phone.

I didn't go to sleep immediately. I lit a cigarette and flipped through *Exclaim!* until I reached filmmaker Bruce LaBruce's audacious column, "Blab," which I anticipated every month like a small child on Christmas morning. For this particular instalment, he related his adventures with his boyfriend, known as "The Muslim," at a fairground and at his parents' house during Thanksgiving. As I read about their month of cotton candy, ecstasy, family and fortune cookies, I knew that I yearned for Yoichi, but I was too stubborn to call him back and admit that maybe I was wrong to stay in Vancouver.

THE GUITAR LESSONS WITH Oliver went better than expected; I was rhythmically challenged and tone-deaf, though knowing this never stopped me from hogging the microphone at karaoke. Somehow, likely because he was a patient and forgiving teacher, I was able to master basic chords. "I can start my own punk band now!" I said the first time I made it through a simple song without faltering. At that moment, I pondered what it might be like to kiss Oliver, but before I could act on the impulse, the phone rang—it was Yoichi. I felt guilty even though nothing had happened.

One day after a lesson, we were sitting in my apartment listening to the Frog Eyes album *The Bloody Hand*, which we were obsessed with at the time. We scanned the listings in *The Georgia Straight* to figure out what we wanted to do that afternoon, vetoing anything that would cost more than fifteen dollars each. After combing through the paper, Oliver wanted to go to the Vancouver Art Gallery to see *The Uncanny: Experiments in Cyborg Culture*, and I agreed to accompany him.

The exhibition contained both art and obsolete technologies: an iron lung, a set of Eadweard Muybridge photographs, a Lee Bul sculpture. As I gazed upon the objects I realized that nearly every person I met was just as anxious about the future as I was. Technology did little to mitigate our fears and our desires, especially after the violence of 9/11.

Once we grew tired of looking at art, we emerged from the gallery onto the street. It was already dark out, but there was enough light for me to see that upon the steps just outside the building, Natalie was sitting with a guy (I recognized him from a local band, but I couldn't recall which one). She had not noticed either of us, but Oliver gazed over and she looked up and there was no avoiding an encounter. Oliver nodded in her direction, seemingly cool, but as she stood up and walked towards us, he grabbed my hand.

"I don't think this is the tactic you want to take. Abort mission!" I whispered, but he ignored me and in seconds she was before us. I freed my hand from his as she leaned over to hug him.

"Julia, this is Natalie," he said, stepping back from her.

"Hello," I said. I tried to smile, but it came out as a grimace.

"You look so familiar," she said to me. "Where do I know you from?"

How many times had we seen each other in the Shaughnessy? Fifteen, twenty times? "I get that a lot," I said, attempting to smile again but failing. "Did you just see the cyborg exhibition?"

"No, Alec and I are just waiting for friends."

"New boyfriend?" Oliver asked.

"Yes."

I could see that Oliver found this news devastating—his hands betrayed his feelings—so I said, "I'm getting a bit cold. We should be on our way. It was lovely to meet you."

We said our goodbyes and departed.

"Will I ever get over her?" Oliver asked as we walked home.

"In another few months you'll wonder why you were so upset."

"It'd be nice to be a cyborg right about now."

"I think I'd rather have feelings," I said.

THE WEATHER IMPROVED AFTER March, but my guitar skills did not. Oliver decided to sublet his apartment and go to Toronto for a few weeks.

"Don't run away," I said.

"I'll be back soon," he said. "I just can't be here right now."

He sent me postcards with short messages about how Natalie was fading from his dreams but that he still could not think about her without experiencing a slight ache in his chest. I wrote back with reports on new tenants and small changes in the building. ("The landlord finally repaired the broken railing on the staircase!") The weeks became months, and I knew there was a chance he wouldn't return. I resumed knitting, determined to perfect a scarf for Yoichi despite the fact that his sojourn in Vancouver was to be over the summer. I made plans with friends I hadn't seen in over half a year. I got a proper haircut. The sadness I was feeling seemed to dissipate.

Soon it was June. One afternoon there was a firm knock at the door. I did not need to check to see who was there—it could only be one person. There, at the entrance of my apartment, stood Yoichi. He looked no different than the day we'd parted at the airport and he smelled the same too. Had nothing changed?

"Julia, I'm home," he said.

I thought about the days ahead of us; his return to London seemed far off and inconsequential. As he entered, the hardwood floor creaked as if to herald his arrival.

Writing in Light

I

CURTIS CALLED ME AT 9:30, waking me. I pretended I had been awake for hours, but he knew better, despite having met me only twice. A few days earlier he had promised he would take me through Jeff Wall's latest New York exhibition before it closed, but we hadn't confirmed our appointment.

"Good morning. I meant to wake you," Curtis said. "I'm at the gallery. They want to shut off the power, so you should arrive on the early side of 10:30. Say 10:15?"

"10:15," I repeated. "See you then."

I removed a book about Robert Smithson from a pile of clothes sitting on a chair so I could find the black dress I wanted to wear. For the last few months, I'd been thinking about Smithson's art, dinosaurs, fossils and skeletons. Somehow I believed that these elements would work in my thesis screenplay, though I wasn't sure what story I was trying to tell.

I dressed quickly. But I was careful to look, as my mother might put it, presentable, in case I needed to deal with a gallery assistant. Girls who sat at the front desk of art galleries scared me, more so than record store clerks once did. Many things frightened me during this time—germs, vampires, suspension bridges—but I feared people the most.

I discovered it was warmer on the street than in my apartment. My room faced a courtyard that didn't get much sunlight. An ex-boyfriend believed that an episode of *Law & Order* had been shot below my window last year. It seemed like there was always a television show or a movie being filmed in our neighbourhood and that I was moving between reality and fantasy whenever I left home.

Although the walk to the 116th Street subway station was a short one, I began to wonder if I would make it to the gallery, located midtown, by 10:15. For a moment I considered taking a taxi, a luxury I could rarely indulge in, but the urge to be economical overrode the need to be on time. I walked to the subway stop and waited on the platform.

The train seemed to take forever to come, a trick of perception. I leaned forward to see if I could spot the lights. It was dark in the tunnel. I began thinking of Jeff Wall's *Double Self-Portrait* (1979).

||

IN *DOUBLE SELF-PORTRAIT*, THE artist looks at us from the corner of his eye. There are two Jeffs in the photograph: one wearing a white shirt with the sleeves rolled up, and one in indigo rinse jeans and a grey sweatshirt with the sleeves pushed back. The Jeff in jeans is wearing a watch. The other Jeff, the one in the white shirt, has his arms crossed, so it's impossible to know if there is a timepiece on either wrist. Behind the two Jeffs is a couch with a pink blanket on it. Jeff with the watch—the one who possesses the technology to measure the passing of time—is touching a papasan chair that's missing its cushion. The chair is white and looks to me like bleached bones in the desert. The man and his doppelgänger are positioned within a room, perhaps located in a building in Vancouver, but that is of little importance. What matters is the look on Jeff's face, the way he is peering out at us peering in at him.

III

ON THE TRAIN, THERE was a sleeping couple sprawled on the seats across from me. During my first semester of grad school I took a photography class with Thomas Roma, who often quoted Robert Frost in his classroom critiques. When I looked at Roma's photographs, even the ones of gospel singers and lovers asleep on the subway, I thought of Frost's poetry.

One afternoon, two days after I cried during his critique of my photographs, Roma told me that he thought writing and photography were the most similar of all the arts. He was certain that taking photographs would help me with my writing; he had once compiled a collection of photographs thinking only of Norman Mailer while he worked.

That night, while reading a textbook for a film theory class, I discovered that *photography* is derived from a Greek word that translates to *writing in light*. This gave me comfort. I concluded that every art form was a way of telling a story—a record of a particular moment in time—even in cases where there was no discernable narrative. Through word and image, I would find a direction for my work: I could write in light.

IV

ANOTHER JEFF WALL WORK: *A Ventriloquist at a Birthday Party in October 1947* (1990).

Red, orange, white, yellow and green helium balloons are touching the living room ceiling, which has a rough texture to it. This is October 1947, the year and month of my father's birth, in muted colour, lit by two lamps.

We are viewing a kid's birthday party. Children are sitting or standing upright, hands clasped in front or behind them. One child is leaning on the arm of a chair. Although all the children are posed differently, their expressions are the same, in clichéd *rapt attention*.

The ventriloquist is a woman with brown hair and a dark coloured dress. Her dummy is male, with brown curls and a shirt with a white ruffled collar. The collar makes me think of fools and Shakespeare or fools in Shakespeare.

In the presence of the ventriloquist, the children forget the snacks and candies: each kid is waiting to hear the words from the dummy's mouth. When the fool speaks, I imagine one of the boys wonders why it sounds so much like the woman with brown hair, the only adult in the room.

V

BACK IN 2002, BEN was renting a room in Jonathan's house on East Cordova Street in the Downtown Eastside. This was before Jonathan and Helen had their baby and there was still a spare bedroom. There were drawings affixed to every surface of the kitchen; both Ben and Jonathan liked sketching pop stars and actors of the moment, and they displayed their work on the refrigerator, on the doors of cupboards and in piles on the table. During this period Nelly, Jennifer Lopez and Ben Affleck figured prominently in their work. Both had a knack of rendering Band-Aids and large diamond rings with a few pencil lines.

Ben and I met at a show. Not an art show. Perhaps it would be clearer if I said *Ben and I met at a concert*. But the word *concert* was too formal for the occasion. Throw in the word *concert* and most people start thinking about Bach or Mozart or even Satie. Then rather than Chucks and jeans and hoodies we're clad in suits and dresses with low necklines, which wasn't the case at all. Perhaps I should have said that Ben and I met while our friends were playing music at the Sugar Refinery, a restaurant/bar/venue where we used to spend a lot of our time. Once, the post-rock band the Beans played a forty-eight-hour show there. I went in the afternoon on the first day and again for the final few hours.

Ben took photographs and I wrote. We were not collaborators, but I think if we were to pool our work, we would have a comprehensive archive of an obscure part of Vancouver's modern history. The Sugar Refinery closed on New Year's Eve 2003, and it seemed as though an era ended with its final show. But even then, I knew six years was nothing when compared to the Mesozoic Era. This was life: over time, we would lose the places and people we loved most.

One afternoon, just before the chill of winter made an outdoor stroll unbearable, Ben and I decided to walk from Vancouver's downtown core to where he lived; further down his street lay the Strathcona neighbourhood. My senses of direction and geography were poor, but I believed that Strathcona, which included Chinatown, was considered a part of downtown Vancouver as well. The distance between point A ("downtown core") and point B ("Jonathan's house") could be measured in minutes: 30 on foot, 7.5 on the buses headed for Powell Street or Nanaimo Station. Our walk lasted longer because we detoured through a park and by a series of fashion warehouses.

Although I'd grown up in the Lower Mainland, I had not spent much time in Strathcona. Other neighbourhoods in Vancouver had become gentrified during the 1990s, but Strathcona remained stubborn to major changes. The first wave of Chinese immigrants and Vietnamese boat people still remained within historic Chinatown, while artists and young families lived on the frontier of industrial zones. Nearby in the Downtown Eastside, there was a series of Single Room Occupancy hotels that were meant to serve as low-income housing but were often in disrepair, creating an environment of seedy despair. Then there were the people that urban planning forgot: homeless men and women drifting from doorways to underground parking lot staircases in search of warmth.

As we walked up to the house, we passed a man standing next to a car. The man's clothes looked like they had been carefully chosen; he stood out in the modest neighbourhood. Ben said hello to the man.

"Who was that?" I asked.

"Oh, he works in the house next door."

"What's next door?"

"A photographer's studio. Do you know Jeff Wall's work?"

VI

THE TRAIN PASSED 86TH Street. I thought about *The Destroyed Room* (1978). The title identifies what the image depicts: a room that has been destroyed. Order has been transformed into disorder.

Judging from the materials strewn about, the room is likely a woman's bedroom. The walls are red. There is a twin mattress with a slash in it. There may have once been a door, but it is gone, leaving the door frame empty. The drawers on a bureau are opened. White fabric peeks out. A hole in the wall reveals soft pink insulation material. The shoes strewn about have heels that tower at a height that, if I were to wear them, would cause me to fall or twist my ankle. Did the woman who lived in this room run in similar shoes to escape from the violence pictured? (Does it matter that, upon closer inspection, the room reveals itself to be a set? That everything I see has been staged?)

It's not the dresses or hats or sunglasses that command my attention. Nor is it the pieces of wood from mismatched furniture scattered about. It is the jewellery that stops me: a strand of translucent orange beads, several plastic orange bracelets, rings made of bone. If I get close enough, I can see earrings. For me, there is something very intimate about jewellery. I marvel at how we let necklaces and bracelets encircle the most vulnerable parts of our bodies and how sometimes we rely on rings to show our love and commitment.

When I first saw this image at the Vancouver Art Gallery, I suddenly knew what photographs could do. I would never look at contemporary art in the same way again. *The Destroyed Room* was created the year I was born.

VII

DURING MY FIRST MONTHS in New York, I spent hours in the darkroom. I liked that I didn't need to talk to anyone when I was there. In the dark there is no need to socialize and fewer opportunities for awkward interactions. Although other people had conversations or listened to music through headphones while making prints, I preferred silence.

Perhaps because I have descended from a long line of manual labourers—butcher, janitor, tailor, nurse—I set aside writing for photography. I was quite sure that some members of my family thought that academia and writing was an excuse to avoid real work. Real work involved heavy lifting or standing, relied on action instead of thought. And although photography had a cerebral element to it, while I was printing photographs I felt like I was labouring: I was doing real work.

The irony that photographs—which rely upon light and exist only because of its presence—must be printed in a darkened room was perfect to me.

VIII

AFTER A PHONE CONVERSATION with Goneril, I had to rethink *A Ventriloquist at a Birthday Party in October 1947*.

Red, orange, white, yellow and green helium balloons are touching the living room ceiling, which has a rough texture to it. This is October 1947, the year and month of my father's birth, in muted colour, lit by two lamps. There is not a television in the room. Goneril explained that this was important because the first television broadcast occurred in October 1947.

"This is a time when a ventriloquist was still an impressive birthday entertainment," she said.

Later I read an essay about the photograph. The woman's voice was supposed to be filtered through the dummy, but because all action was stilled, there was only silence.

I couldn't remember an impressive birthday party of my own, though I knew my parents did their best each year and there were cakes and presents. Even at age twenty-six, I thought I might like to see a ventriloquist perform.

IX

I GOT OFF AT Columbus Circle, double-checking the address and directions I had written down. I was looking for the Marian Goodman Gallery.

I checked the time, calculating that I'd be five minutes late when I reached my destination. As I walked across Central Park South, avoiding the horse manure on the street, I marvelled at the fact that I was in New York, a city that had once existed only in books, television and movies for me.

The Marian Goodman Gallery was located in a building that housed a number of other art dealers. As I rode the elevator, I realized that I had read an article about Goodman in *The New Yorker* a few months earlier. All I remembered from the piece was that she had refused to relocate to Chelsea. At times, her staff had no choice but to remove the front windows of the gallery in order to accommodate works too large for the industrial-sized elevator.

The elevator doors opened directly into the gallery. Curtis and three other men were crouched next to a small piece, which was on the floor on top of a sheet. The larger works were still mounted on the wall in their lightboxes. A few of the photographs were unlit and I worried that they had already shut off the power.

Curtis saw me and flicked a switch, restoring the electricity. The room became illuminated by scenes from the Pacific Northwest. The photographs contained the landscape and architecture that defined the city I called home. I had not known that I was capable of feeling homesick until then.

I walked to a photograph of a Stó:lō excavation. One man was digging while another was looking on. My thoughts on bones and culture and excavation and history and the place I was from loomed before me, in a succinct image. I thought of Robert Pickton, the serial killer who had preyed upon women who lived or worked in the Downtown Eastside. There were so many bones and teeth scattered across his pig farm that it required a large team of forensic anthropologists to excavate the site.

I slowly made my way through the rooms of the gallery. Curtis pointed out a controversial photograph of a bloody rag situated on the ground outside Wall's studio. Critics at the European show had hated it. In my state, I was enamoured with the piece.

When I was about to leave, I thanked Curtis for letting me into the gallery. I told him I was excited by the fact that I saw the photographs in both their dark and illuminated states. We talked about an essay a film scholar wrote about Wall's photographs when they were not lit. Then Curtis led me to a lightbox containing a photograph of two boys crossing into a graveyard. The sides of the lightbox frame were off, allowing us to look behind the transparency. There were dozens of fluorescent light tubes lined up vertically.

Curtis looked at me, and in a moment that sounded scripted he said, "You're looking at the bones of the piece."

Sad Ghosts

"UNSCIENTIFIC," GENE SAID, SMACKING his hand against the bar top. "Do you really believe it's necessary for film crews shooting in Hong Kong to make offerings to placate the gods? That a roast pig and a bottle of cheap alcohol will keep the doctor away? Don't try to bring up *The Dark Knight* and Heath Ledger's death and Edison Chen's sex scandal as proof that omitting a superstitious ritual will result in tragedy. If you were building a house upon this sorry excuse for a foundation, the structure would disintegrate within a year of completion."

"Science is just another way of telling a story," I said. "It's a narrative. Conflict and resolution. Man versus nature."

A shadow ghosted itself across Gene's face, something like doubt.

"I find that cities by water seem most haunted," I said, knowing this statement would provoke him.

Gene snorted.

"That's an ugly sound," I said. "Have you not experienced something inexplicable? Something beyond measurement and calibration?"

"Are you a Creationist? A Holocaust denier?" He sneered. The man sitting next to him glanced over at us, mouth open as if he was about to speak, but he chose to say nothing.

"This line of reasoning is unbecoming," I said in an even tone of voice, not wanting to succumb to indignation.

"I have never experienced a supernatural disturbance, and I have spent my life living in cities situated near bodies of water: LA, New

York and Hong Kong," Gene said to me. To the bartender he said, "Another round."

"Do you remember Andy?" I asked. "We once ran into him at the movie theatre at IFC when we went to see *Black Swan*."

"Is he that lanky sneakerhead who gives the impression that he's afraid to live?"

"That's not a very generous description, but I suppose you're right. He lets fear dictate all his decisions. Once, he asked me to help him break up with a girlfriend—a very good friend of mine—because of his aversion to conflict. Anyhow, I don't think I've told you that Andy can only hear ghosts rather than see them. I guess instead of *yin yang* eyes, he has *yin yang* ears if that's even a thing. Once, he was standing in a kitchen in an apartment on the sixth floor of a *tong lau* at 65 Peel Street and a knife slid across the counter and someone was whispering in Shanghainese—the speaker's syntax and vocabulary seemed to indicate that he had died sometime during the early 1940s. Andy said he knew that the ghost had a moustache—a full beard, even—and that the spirit wasn't malevolent, just lost."

"That seems anachronistic," Gene said. "None of the Shanghai emigrants to Hong Kong during that era had facial hair."

"How do you know?" I asked.

"I just know. I *read*."

"So do I."

"Did you know that most so-called hauntings are likely due to infrasound?" Gene asked.

"What's that?"

"It's when the frequency of sound is less than twenty hertz per second. One study suggests it causes some people to feel awe or fear, or to interpret an environment as being somewhat odd or inhabited by supernatural entities."

"Interesting," I said. "But it doesn't account for instances of seeing spirits. Just last week Stephanie and I were at the *dai pai dong* on Elgin waiting for our food when a man sat down and said to me, 'I have not been here in over twenty years.'

"'What brought you out tonight?' I asked because I had the feeling he needed to talk and he had no one to talk to. He told me he had just visited a friend, and that he used to live at number seventy-seven. I told him I hadn't eaten there either since I left the neighbourhood just shy of a year earlier.

"The man told me his apartment at seventy-seven Elgin was haunted. When he first moved in, the mirror in the living room was painted over. He said he should have known that because it had been intentionally covered up, something was wrong. Yet, despite his reservations, he removed the paint. The process took three days—the paint was layered on, red and foreboding. Then he started seeing things in the mirror. First, it was just mist: dark patches that could be blamed on night vision or dirt. One evening, he saw a ghost with long hair, a white dress and no feet hovering in the glass as if she was standing next to him.

"Although I was fascinated with this story, I ran out of language to interrogate the man further, plus Stephanie doesn't understand Cantonese so it seemed kind of rude for me to continue to talk to this stranger. The food arrived and I waited for the man to leave before I translated the conversation for her. I hate the feeling of being talked about in a language I don't speak.

"Stephanie told me that while she was watching us talk she felt as if she was experiencing a scene out of a Wong Kar-wai movie. Although the man didn't get into it, I imagined that the apparition's hair was thick and black, but the strands separated at the end so that if you weren't too afraid to look closely, you could count each strand one by one."

"I wouldn't be afraid to look because there would be nothing to see," said Gene.

"So anyway, Andy was telling me a story about two of his colleagues, a married man and a single woman," I said. "He loathed both but had to work closely with them on a marketing project. Something dull—I've forgotten the details. He described them as two people with little imagination and a crippling inability to tell a story. I think Andy would have preferred it if they were pathological liars, because then at least their conversations would have been thrilling and unsettling.

"But one night this pair was working late or having some sort of clandestine affair under the guise of industrious productivity. Their office was located in a mostly empty industrial building on the eighteenth floor. They entered the elevator a few minutes before midnight. The elevator began to descend, but before they reached the ground level, the doors opened up on the fourth floor. The space had been gutted some months before and was partway through a renovation."

At this point, the bartender delivered our drinks. I took a sip of mine to quell the itchiness I was feeling in my throat.

"So what was on the fourth floor?" I continued. "Nothing. There was only blackness; no one was waiting for the elevator. Then a bluish light appeared in the distance and it began to grow until the couple could see that a blue-hued woman was flying towards them. Her hair and clothing flowed behind her as if the speed she was moving at was creating its own wind. They screamed like little schoolgirls and hit the 'close' button rapidly. The doors shut just as the spirit was about to enter the compartment. I don't think they've worked late since then."

"At best, your description of what happened is something out of a third-rate Japanese horror film, and at worst it is some kind of banal moralistic tale in which two people having an affair are punished by supernatural forces."

"Sometimes I wonder why I subject myself to your company," I said.

"I keep you honest," he said.

"Were you living in New York when the Met had that exhibition about photography and the occult?" I asked. "I think it was called *The Perfect Medium*. Put your phone down—don't Google this. Can't we have a conversation where we rely solely on our memories?"

Gene scowled at me, but he complied with my request. "Yes, I was in New York at that time and I saw that show," he said.

"What did you think about the spirit photographs from the 1860s?"

"They're proof that a grieving person will believe anything. That genre of photography peaked shortly after the American Civil War, and regained popularity after the First World War. Wives and daughters were willing to overlook the possibility of double exposure. They believed that their departed loved ones were really appearing in spirit form in photographs with them. Photographers such as William H. Mumler were just opportunists preying upon people who lost husbands and fathers and sons."

"See, I knew that your powers of recall would be up to this challenge."

"I have science in my corner. Meanwhile, you have yet to sway me with any of your anecdotes."

"Would it help if I told you a personal story?" I asked.

"Why not? You've failed so far, so you may as well try a new tactic."

"When I was eight," I said, "my parents sent me to an art day camp that was located near a lake. By the lake was a cluster of Edwardian country homes, including one called Ceperley House, which was designed by the English architect R.P.S. Twizell and built in 1911 on land adjacent to a strawberry farm. Henry and Grace Ceperley named their home *Fairacres*. At the time it was the biggest house in the area, and it proved expensive to run.

"Once Grace died, the mansion served as a tuberculosis ward for Vancouver General Hospital—a fact that is omitted from official literature on the history of the house—then was home to a Benedictine order of monks. Some years later, an American man named William Franklin Wolsey was on the run from charges of bigamy, assault and extortion and he ended up in Burnaby and bought the house and started a cult called the Temple of the More Abundant Life. This too is not part of the official narrative about the house. Wolsey fled the country in 1960. A few years later, Simon Fraser University repurposed the building as a dormitory. At that time, students organized a series of sit-ins. Once, during a protest, someone set a bonfire upon the hardwood floor of the billiard room.

"I knew the house as the Burnaby Art Gallery. As part of the art camp, we went to see an exhibition at Ceperley House. I think it was a show of paintings—I'm not too clear about that because the work didn't make an impression on me. We left to go back to the sculpture studio. As I was walking across a field, I turned to look back at the house. A greenish figure with long, dark hair was standing behind a window, waving at me. I looked away, and when I glanced back the apparition was still there, waving.

"That day, I didn't tell anyone what I had seen, but some years later I returned during a class trip and asked a gallery assistant whether they had ever placed anything in the windows of the house and I was given a strange look and told, 'No, we would never do anything like that.'"

"I believe that you believe that this happened," Gene said.

"Okay, it's your turn," I said, unwilling to surrender without mounting one more offensive. "You must have had an experience laced with horror—everyone has at least one story."

Gene paused. A chill came over me. I looked up and saw that I was sitting directly below an air-conditioning vent.

"Last year, one of my young cousins died very suddenly," he said, staring into his tumbler of whisky. "My aunt was destroyed by her death. Her doctor put her on antidepressants and she was sleeping all the time. My dad was really worried, but he was manifesting his anxieties as anger towards me so I didn't even call him on Father's Day. It didn't help that two of my cousin's high school classmates also died on the same night. Three families were grieving, and you know how I get when there's so much emotion—I'm uncomfortable. It gets so bad I don't even know where to put my hands when I'm trying to have a conversation. I just wanted to do something to make things right again.

"I was looking at pictures on Facebook from the last week of my cousin's life," Gene continued. "She and her friends had gone to a flat on Lantau for a weekend and they had taken a lot of pictures. The strange thing was that there were all these warped photos—their faces were all distorted like they had been messing around with effects on Photobooth. So I decided to visit that rental flat to see if I could find any answers about her death. It was a crumbling sort of place littered with Jurassic technologies. Instead of a DVD player, there was a VCR. On the first night it rained and I was stuck indoors, bored and cursing myself for forgetting to bring a book. At the time I was in the middle of *The Immortal Life of Henrietta Lacks*. If you haven't read it, you must."

"I've read it," I said. "It's an incredible book."

"So this was how I came to search through the VHS collection for something to watch," said Gene. "There were a number of trite romantic comedies. You know how much I detest that genre—I find it so juvenile. I was drawn to an unmarked tape in a plain white box and soon I found myself watching what I can only describe as a weird short film."

I shivered and wrapped my shawl over the top of my head.

"The opening shot is of the moon, obscured by clouds," Gene continued. "Then a mirror shows a woman who is combing her hair. There is a jump cut and then the woman is looking behind her. Her body language communicates fear. From there, the visuals become even stranger. Chinese characters drift around the screen. Then there is a scene with people crawling along the ground. A man with a sheet over his head and face appears, his right arm stretched out as if he is giving directions. Then, there is a close-up of an eye. The film ends with an image in a forest. There are dead leaves blanketing the ground, and in the centre of the shot there is a well.... The screen went snowy at this point, as if the film had been interrupted. Right when I turned off the TV, the phone in the flat rang. But there was no one on the line."

"Wait, isn't this the plot of *Ringu*?" I asked. A feeling of outrage crept from my chest up my throat.

"Yes, it's *fiction*, much like all of the stories you've told me tonight."

"You're such a dick."

"What were you expecting?"

"I don't know. I didn't think you were capable of this kind of adaptation and embellishment," I said.

"So, did you help Andy break up with your friend?"

"I can't believe you would ask me that."

"So, did you?"

How Does a Single Blade of Grass
Thank the Sun?

MY DRAGOONS AND I were gathered to discuss our plans for neigh-bourhood domination. Yellow Peril, The Chairman, Suzie Wrong, Riceboy and I, the Sick Man of Asia, converged every Friday night to chop suey like a group of triad bosses. Chingers, all of us. Slanty-eyed teenage disappointments with no better place to haunt but the schoolyard near the abode of my *ma ma* and *ba ba*.

Tags covered the walls of our institution of mediocre learning. Every overzealous territory marker in the area had hit the walls like vicious dogs, making it difficult to discern that the school had once been grey. The poor spelling that appeared in most of the graffiti was evidence of the region's subpar education system; the choice was not a self-aware homage to hip hop influences. To one-up all the noddies and ain't-gonna-ever-bes, last winter The Chairman had stencilled OBEY MAO on the basketball court blacktop. He even included an image based on the portrait of Mao at Tiananmen Square, but the only thing that looked right in The Chairman's version was Mao's giant mole, located on his chin. Some of the neighbourhood children thought the tag said OBEY YAO; they had a rather limited knowledge of history, no respect for our people's illustrious past.

The Chairman and I had a re-education program for the neigh-bourhood youths, which consisted primarily of lectures and rigorous beatings. We enjoyed thrashing sense into the ignorant youngsters. The Chairman elected to go the Bruce Lee way of the empty hand, while I preferred the traditional tools of corporal punishment.

Nothing pleased me more than placing a dunce cap on an eight-year-old simpleton's head, while making jokes about dimwits and slow learners and applying the strap to tender hands. Riceboy took offence to this, which was why he refused to partake in the re-education scheme—he had been subjected to ESL classes during elementary school despite his fluency in the language of the colonizer.

Anyhow, the stupider the children were, the harder we would hit them. The Chairman and I made the little noddies stand in urine-stained corners, holding their ears, while we unleashed our fury upon them. No mercy for the retards, either. The Chairman didn't stand for any PC bullshit. "We're equal opportunity," he once said while smacking a child whose IQ was reported to be in the low seventies. "Retards are kids, too. Why should we make them feel lesser than their fellow nose-picking classmates? They should be included in all the reindeer games. As you know, I'm anti-exclusionary policy."

My own mantra while administering lashings with the feather duster was, "I'm doing this for you, not for me." This was my *ma ma's* favourite phrase, and she was a wise woman. Anything good enough for me was good enough for that lot of simpletons and punks. From time to time I considered asking my *ma ma* to etch those very words on my back so I could have my own version of the story of Yueh Fei, one of my favourite heroes of Chinese history. I imagined that, like him, I was on a mission to save my country.

On this particular Friday night we were gathered without an agenda. The previous week we had screened *Hero* and *The Emperor and the Assassin*, much to the delight of The Chairman, who believed in the first emperor's concept of *tianxia*. On this point he and Yellow Peril differed. Peril's family was Taiwanese and she believed with occidental-eyed earnestness that someday Taiwan would "liberate China from Communism."

At the end of that evening, Riceboy and I had to physically restrain Peril—she was ready to get all assassin on The Chairman. I have to say, touching her arm got my heart beating all allegro-like, but I wasn't ready to act on those feelings.

This week, a showdown between me and Riceboy was playing out. Riceboy was getting ready to chop friend because I had said that

Johnnie To had surpassed John Woo as an action director.

"You have to admit that John Woo has the most *ging* shootouts," Riceboy said, adjusting the giant gold chain around his neck.

"I'm not dismissing Woo," I said. "I often dream of the day he remakes *Le Cercle Rouge* with Tony Leung Chiu-Wai as the Alain Delon character and Fatty Chow as the alcoholic marksman. It's just that..."

"Are you *still* trying to get the whole 'Fatty Chow' thing to catch on?" Suzie asked. "Chow Yun-Fat is famous in the West now. People know who he is. He's been in a zillion Hollywood films."

"The *A Better Tomorrow* years are still upon me," I said in my defence, even though I could sense that The Chairman was growing bored of our conversation. He considered the Cantonese cinema a bourgeois diversion and refused to acknowledge its existence.

"The *Bulletproof Monk* years, more like it," Riceboy scoffed.

Suzie Wrong started girl-talking with Yellow Peril separate from the group. I thought I heard my name, so I leaned in a fraction, but they were speaking at such a low decibel that I could not eavesdrop. I wanted to agitate Suzie Wrong, all ninety pounds of her. I wanted to cause something of a scene so that Yellow Peril would engage with me, even if only to defend Suzie. So for lack of Einstein conversation, I started water-torturing Riceboy on his *nom de guerre*.

"Why'd you choose such a dickless name?" I said, spitting on the ground with gusto, just like I'd seen those coolie-types and fresh-off-the-boats do in Middle Kingdom Town. I was practising to be the best possible Chinaman I could be, embracing the vices as well as the virtues with equal dedication.

"The Sick Man of Asia? How's that any better?" Riceboy hiked up his giant pants, which were riding so low they would have revealed his boxer shorts, except he was wearing a T-shirt that nearly reached his knees. He was taller than me and had a twenty-five-pound advantage, but his style choices were a definite handicap in a fight.

"It's a reclamation," I said. "I've taken the slang of the West and altered the meaning for my own usage, thereby exercising a certain mastery over the language of the colonizer. So I ask again, why'd you choose such a dickless name?"

"Chigga, what?" Riceboy raised his fists at me.

"Why do you have to emasculate him?" demanded Suzie Wrong. Apparently she had been listening to us the whole time, despite her side conversation with Peril. "You say dickless as if it were an insult."

It took the kind of willpower it takes to wake up every morning before dawn to tend a rice field to keep me from smiling. I had her attention, which meant I had Yellow Peril's as well. My heart beat faster, as if I'd won a giant stuffed animal doing something manly at the carnival.

"Yeah, Sick. I don't feel the lack," Yellow Peril chimed in, thrusting her pelvis forward. I noticed that she was wearing a very fetching pair of knee-high boots. I wanted to get up in her lack, so I feigned interest in her words. I nodded.

The Chairman looked at me slantways. Even in his pyjama-like costume he stank of authority. I tolerated his propaganda mongering because he meant well. Our views on the Motherland differed, but we lived in Lotusland, so that was the tit we had to suck on. No use in raging over petty details and ideologies, especially since the Chairman believed that Riceboy and I were colonized dogs who were resistant to the Chinese voice of reason. The Chairman always had the advantage—his family was from the Mainland, while my family, as well as Riceboy's, hailed from Hong Kong.

"The name fits with the nomenclature, comrade," The Chairman said.

Finally, Riceboy spoke. He opted to unleash his flawless Cantonese. "*I hope your sons are born without asses.*" The ultimate curse.

I spat on the ground, and held back a sigh. Yes, I had insulted his manhood, even though I knew from experience how difficult it was to be a yellow man in the new world. I should have known better. Yet, I resented his words—I had insulted him as an individual while he had insulted my family to be. But instead of confronting him, I opted to redirect the evening.

"Silencio," I said. "Order, order, and all that. What is our business this fine spring night?"

"Chaos and destruction," said Yellow Peril. The way she said it made me worship her all the more. I started imagining what she looked like naked. I wondered if she had freckles on her tits, or if she had funny tan lines from her bikini.

"Excellent," I said, snapping out of my daydream. "What to destroy, now that is the question."

"No pillaging," insisted Riceboy, tugging on the waistband of his jeans.

"That's something I can't guarantee, Liceboy," I said, cooliefying my English, still a little sore that he'd cursed my unborn children.

Last week, to divert attention away from the feud between Peril and The Chairman, I had suggested we trespass upon the Riceboy family laundry. I thought we could smash a couple of stereotypes in the process. Riceboy did not find this funny in the least. He told me that my ideas were stupid. *Ideas.* As in, all of them, not just this particular one. Yeah, he was sore about the whole thing, so sore that he had become a festering week-old wound.

The laundry business had existed for three generations. It had history, the kind that inspires Lotusland novelists to fill reams of paper with stories featuring multigenerational conflict and politically correct resolution. Riceboy's parents thought he would take over once he completed an MBA. One thing about him that I envied: his clothes always looked clean and neatly pressed, even if they were a bit roomy.

The Chairman sensed tension between us and decreed, "Let's make like SARS and spread."

So we got in Riceboy's rice rocket—a vehicle recognizable at a hundred paces because of its magnificent spoiler and dozens of anime figurines populating the ledge next to the rear window—and he rickshawed us through the wet Lotusland streets.

"Let's go to Middle Kingdom Town," Suzie suggested.

Riceboy floored it. He was excellent behind the wheel, a regular Tokyo-drifting god, which was why I had appointed him our official driver months earlier. Also, he was the only one of us who didn't have to ask his parents' permission to borrow the family car.

Ten minutes later, we arrived at our destination. Middle Kingdom Town was crowded, a real picture of humanity. There were the coolies, the FOBS, the Lotusland-born and the tourists. Oh, how I detested the tourists. They looked for authenticity in a place that could not provide it. Middle Kingdom Town could not stand in for the Motherland. My dragoons and I knew this well. But there were fools who thought that thousands of years of culture could be compressed into the poorest neighbourhood in the city.

As we walked down Pender, I noticed Scott Wilson, who is sick with yellow fever, standing next to hundreds of little toys. He was flirting with the girl selling them. I imagined he was complimenting her camel toe, saying, "Baby, I love how tight your jeans are. Let me give you herpes."

"Hey, three-inch egg roll boy!" he shouted when he saw me. He grabbed his crotch and made a big production of insulting me. The beads in his Buddhist bracelet clattered. For a moment I thought he was going to whip out his penis and a measuring tape to prove his worth in inches. Lucky for all in the vicinity of Middle Kingdom Town, he kept his little boy in his pants.

Scott's hostility was deep-rooted. The situation was this: last month he asked Suzie Wrong out on a date. Well, he asked her for a lot more than that, but I'm a gentleman and not some gossip-mongering auntie hunched over a mah-jong table, so I'll stick to the date euphemism. Suzie had no interest ("Not even if I had AIDS and no one else wanted to touch my sick ass," she confided to me later) and told him as politely as she could, no. Then he said, "It's in your Asian genes to be a whore or mail-order bride or work at a massage parlour."

"You forgot about nail-salon technician," she deadpanned, not losing her cool for a moment. Scott nodded, thinking that he had scored points with Suzie. He was the biggest simpleton that we knew, dimmer than poor Edward Yip, who had suffered some raging fever as an infant and processed thoughts at the pace of a dial-up internet connection.

When I heard about this incident, I threatened to de-man Scotty boy, make a Rice Queen out of him. I told him that he was cruising for a Bobbitting. This took him a day to decipher because he didn't have any older sisters who remembered with filtered-water clarity the current events of the nineties. When he finally figured out what I'd meant after some sleuthing on the internet, he chose to put a brick through the windshield of Riceboy's rice rocket with a note attached that said YOUR CHINK ASS IS SO DEAD. "Sorry, Riceboy," I said when I saw the damage. "I guess we *all look same.*"

"Hey, villain," I said to Scott, ignoring the insult to my manhood. "Confucius say *diu lei lo mo.*"

Scott looked confused. No amount of studying Suzie Wrong's ass could prepare him for non-English insults. None of the other Chingers liked him, so he didn't know the choice swears of any dialect.

"Whatever, egg roll boy," he muttered, unable to produce a fresh insult. "Ching chong ching chong, motherfucker." The expression on his face was comical. He seemed confused and afraid and violent and entitled all at once. His mouth was agape. The girl at the toy stand shot me an amused glance. She knew the mother tongue. My dragoons whooped. Victory! We sauntered past, and stepped into The Noodle Shop.

Once inside, we got our own table. No sharing for us since we were five. The waitress came up to us and said, "What do you want?" No hello, no how are you tonight. This was how things were done in Middle Kingdom Town. The masochist in me enjoyed this treatment very much. Plus, we could get away with tipping far less than fifteen percent.

I ordered a red bean ice and fried egg sandwich, Suzie had a half and half and dumplings, Peril wanted fish balls and noodles, The Chairman refused to eat in public, and Riceboy, well, he had fried rice and a Diet Coke.

"What's wrong with sugar?" I asked.

"Chigga, what?" Riceboy glowered at me.

"You heard me. What's wrong with sugar?" I hit his can of Diet Coke with a pair of chopsticks.

"Why you have to be that way, *son?*"

"Your chigga accent does us no favours," I said. "Why do you have to appropriate another culture when you speak? We have our own trials and tribulations to draw from. We don't have to pilfer the pain of others in order to achieve some kind of authenticity."

The food arrived, ending the conversation.

I was hard on Riceboy because I loved him like the brother I didn't have—I had two older sisters. My parents tried very hard to have me, precious son, keeper of the family name. Or so they said, but they seemed rather disinterested in me. It was as if they had exhausted their all-star parenting skills on my sisters. One was a doctor and the other a lawyer. Suffice to say, they were prime specimens, a credit, as it were, to the race. That's what our neighbour said last year. She's ninety, so instead of leaving a bag of burning dogshit on her front porch, I forgave her for being an ignoramus.

I looked around the table. Yellow Peril was slurping up her noodles with gusto. Riceboy was shovelling rice into his mouth like a champion competitive eater, while Suzie Wrong took big gulps of her drink. The Chairman looked on as if he was posing for a painting. I was poking at the red beans in my glass. We had so much potential, but sometimes it seemed as if we would amount to nothing. It was clear—my dragoons and I needed a little structure in our lives. We needed to achieve a goal of some sort.

"We must do something tonight," I said. "We need an activity."

"Cat burglary!" Yellow Peril suggested.

"Revolution," The Chairman said.

"What we need, dear friends, is a heist," I said.

"What about the mural?" asked Yellow Peril. There was a mural down by one of the beaches that we wanted to paint over. We talked about doing this at least once a month. The mural depicted the joys of colonial life, roughing it in the wilderness, and the triumph of the settlers over the natives. We wanted to remove the near-naked depictions of First Nations people (the region was far too cold for the skimpy traditional costumes pictured, of this I was almost sure) and paint moustaches on all the settlers.

"We don't have any paint," I said.

"There's a ton of leftover paint at my house," Suzie said. "My parents just painted the kitchen. There should be enough left for our purposes."

"Excellent," I said.

We paid the bill, leaving a ten-percent tip, and walked out onto the sidewalk. The air was cool and smelled clean, like rain. It was a perfect Lotusland night.

We got in the rice rocket and sped towards Suzie's house. The thing about Suzie is that her surname is Wong, but her first name isn't really Suzie. Her parents are not so lacking in English skills or understanding of Western popular culture to give her the same name as a fictional hooker.

When we reached the Wong residence, I gave out a series of commands. "Suzie, show Riceboy and The Chairman where the paint is. They'll carry it back."

The three left the car. My plan had worked. I was alone with Yellow Peril.

"So, Peril, did you just get your hair cut?" I asked, brushing a lock of hair away from her face. I knew the answer, because I had overheard Peril telling Suzie all about her genius Japanese stylist.

"Yesterday," she said, touching her hair. I noticed that she had on a bright red lip gloss that made her mouth look like a delicious hard candy.

"You look fetching," I said. I was all ready to move in for the kill, to lean in and kiss her shellac shiny lips when Riceboy threw the door open.

"Am I interrupting something?" He smirked knowingly, and slid into the driver's seat. He let a big fart rip, and it had the unfortunate characteristics of being both loud and stinky.

I sighed. Peril opened the door to get some air. I really had to mend my relationship with Riceboy. If I didn't do anything, he would continue on like this, acting as if he was just goofing things up by mistake, all the while pulling up his pants. There would always be an edge of malice in all his dealings with me if I didn't apologize in some way.

After The Chairman loaded the cans of paint, rollers, pans and brushes into the trunk, we headed to the beach.

Riceboy shredded the scenic route, motoring down narrow streets that had a view of the ocean and the mountains. I peered at my friends again, examining their faces and slouched postures. These were my dragoons. In the moonlight they looked like the kind of people to whom the poets of yesteryear would dedicate verse.

Riceboy halted the car. We had arrived. We were ready to launch.

I got out, popped the trunk and put a drop cloth over the back licence plate. I'd eyeballed enough movies to be an expert on side-stepping issues with the law. Riceboy draped his oversized coat over the front plate. The Chairman marched the cans of paint over to the mural, and Peril and Suzie gathered the remaining supplies.

We approached the mural with the fanfare of a winning army, whooping and menacing our way down the path. The mural had a sinister vibe. Under the streetlight, the settlers appeared to have leers upon their faces. They looked like zombies or cannibals or vampires or some type of unknown monster that fed on the flesh of humans.

"It's really in need of a touch-up," Suzie said.

Everyone nodded in agreement.

The Chairman filled a pan with paint, then another. Peril handed me a roller. Riceboy and Suzie grabbed the brushes. We were not jibber-jabbering, but somehow we had all sidled up to the same conclusion: we were going to paint over the entire mural.

We laboured like the Chingers that we were, and in less than an hour, the task was finito.

"That summer you spent slaving for that painting company was worth it," I said to Riceboy. "This is an example of fine craftsmanship." Despite all that had transpired that night, the corners of my mouth pulled up—a smile. Riceboy's face held the same expression. I imagined that this was forgiveness, or something like it.

Peril was next to me, an opportunity. I got up in her personal space, and seized her hand. Her hair smelled like a field of wild flowers, and I was a bee wanting to gather her pollen. She didn't treat me like a leper. Instead, she held my hand like it was a giant wad of cash she was afraid to drop.

The wall was now beige, slick like the Wongs' kitchen. There was no evidence that there had once been a mural. My dragoons and I gazed at the blank slate before us. Light drizzle began to fall, but we continued to stand at attention. Although it's said that the Great Wall of China is the only manmade thing visible from space, at that moment it felt as if anyone looking down upon the Earth would have seen that expanse of beige wall, and us, sleeping giants shaking off a long slumber, presiding over it.

Acknowledgements

REALLY, HOW DOES A single blade of grass thank the sun? It took me a very long time to write this book. I had a lot of support and guidance along the way.

Thank you to my family, and to Elizabeth Bachinsky, Liz Byer, Annie Choi, Kevin Chong, Joe Clark, Amber Dawn, Rilla Friesen, Jacob Gelfand, Andrea Gin, Rebecca Godfrey, Bethanne Grabham, John High, Carmen Johnson, Anna Ling Kaye, Helen Kim, Bourree Lam, Sarah Lebo, H.J. Lee, Samantha Leese, Sylvia Legris, Ming Kai Leung, Janey Lew, Andrea Libin, Maloy Luakian, Robyn Marshall, Jada Pape, Ed Park, Aaron Peck, Meredith & Peter Quartermain, Kate Reilly, Karen Russell, Jeremy Takada Balden, Zena Sharman, Silas White and Diane Williams. Many thanks to Carleton Wilson for his magnificent book design.

I owe a great debt to all my classmates and the professors of my writing workshops and seminars at the University of British Columbia, Lancaster University and Columbia University. Thank you to Sue Ann Alderson, Lynne Bowen, Kate Braid, Jonathan Dee, Francisco Goldman, George Green, Paul Lafarge, Sam Lipsyte, Murray Logan, Sigrid Nunez, George McWhirter, Keith Maillard, Ben Marcus, Maureen Medved and Stephen O'Connor. I'd also like to thank the Writers' Trust of Canada, Spring Workshop and Witte de With Contemporary Art for their support.

The following stories were previously published: "Days of Being Wild" in *Ricepaper*; "How Does a Single Blade of Grass Thank the Sun?" in *Event* and *The Journey Prize Stories 25*; "Left and Leaving" in *Zen Monster*; "O, Woe Is Me" in *Grain*; "Rerun" in *Grain*; "Robot by the River" in *Day One*; "Sad Ghosts" in *A Fictional Residency*; and "Two-Part Invention" in *Grain*.

About the Author

DORETTA LAU IS A journalist who covers arts and culture for *Artforum International*, *South China Morning Post*, *The Wall Street Journal Asia* and *LEAP*. She completed an MFA in Writing at Columbia University. Her fiction and poetry have appeared in *Day One*, *Event*, *Grain Magazine*, *Prairie Fire*, *PRISM International*, *Ricepaper*, *sub-TERRAIN* and *Zen Monster*. She splits her time between Vancouver and Hong Kong, where she is at work on a novel and a screenplay. In 2013, she was a finalist for the Writers' Trust of Canada / McClelland & Stewart Journey Prize.

PHOTO: MING KAI LEUNG